Parlez-Vous Murder?

Susan Kiernan-Lewis

Other books by Susan Kiernan-Lewis

Crime and Croissants
Accent on Murder
A Bad Éclair Day
Free Falling
Going Gone
Heading Home
Blind Sided
Rising Tides
Cold Comfort
Never Never
Wit's End
Dead On
Murder in the South of France
Murder à la Carte
Murder in Provence
Murder in Paris
Murder in Aix
Murder in Nice
Murder in the Latin Quarter
Murder in the Abbey
Murder in the Bistro
Murder in Cannes
Swept Away
Carried Away
Stolen Away
Reckless
Shameless
Breathless
Heartless
Clueless
Hopeless

Parlez-Vous Murder?

Book 1 of the
Stranded in Provence Mysteries

Susan Kiernan-Lewis

Susan Kiernan-Lewis

San Marco Press, Atlanta
Copyright 2017

1

A Moment in Time

I'm pretty sure when I write about this later I'm going to say there were signs.

I'm probably going to pinpoint the feeling of prescient dread that sparked the air that June morning as I threw back the duvet on the bed in my borrowed apartment in the village of Chabanel outside Aix-en-Provence.

I'll probably mention that there were no birds singing when I awoke and how I thought that was foreboding. I'll definitely point out how yellow the sky was when I set out on my walk to the village café for my morning java.

But none of that is true.

The fact is I had no idea what that day would bring. I did in fact walk to the village *boulangerie* for a much anticipated almond croissant, but the clouds were puffy and white and skittered across a dazzling azure sky.

The croissant itself was flaky and exploded in my mouth in an exquisite rush of sugar and butter. In fact, if I'm honest, that morning was the first happy moment I'd had in six months.

There was simply no indication at all that the world as I knew it was about to end.

But I digress. Allow me to take you back to the beginning of my story which started with a seriously crappy moment in my life-up-until-then and how I unfortunately reacted to it.

First let me just say that I have lived through a few crappy moments in my life.

I once slept through my alarm on the morning I was to take my law school entrance exam and by the time they could reschedule me I'd broken my leg skiing and had to reschedule *again* so that by the time I finally sat for the exam I was so far removed from the time I'd studied for it that I totally and truly bombed it. And while at the time my mother reminded me that there was always Trinidad Law School, by then I was out of the mood of being a lawyer.

The point is, I've had a few bad things happen to me in my thirty-four years but nothing, *nothing*, compared to the moment I arrived at my boyfriend Gilbert's condo in Atlanta all aglow with the euphoric certainty that he was about to propose to me only to hear his perfectly logical reasons for why we should break up.

I suppose I should have seen it coming but, as usual, my mind was somewhere else. It was busy picking out Pottery Barn drapes for the Buckhead townhouse in which I imagined I'd be living with Gilbert. It was sorting through the exact verbiage for my engagement announcement on The Knot and Weddings.com and it was busy relishing the expressions of covetous envy on the faces of my closest girl pals when they heard the news.

In case I haven't made it clear, I have a tendency to jump several months—or sometimes years—ahead of where I really am in life and somehow along the way the interim gets lost. Someone talking about living in the present?

You might as well be speaking Urdu to me.

Anyway, somehow I'd jumped over the *now* part of my relationship with Gilbert and had moved on at warp speed to the—at least in my mind—inevitable *marriage* part.

I'll admit this tendency of mine is a definite character flaw and one I intend to work very hard to eliminate in the future. In the meantime however, after the above-mentioned shock of being on the totally opposite wavelength as Gilbert I decided to use one of the two tickets I'd bought months earlier for a surprise birthday trip to the south of France with Gilbert to get out of town to clear my head and begin the tiresome process of getting over Gilbert.

I know that sounds very logical and, trust me, very unlike me, but full disclosure: it was a house swap that had been arranged months earlier and frankly I couldn't get out of it.

The flight itself was moderately endurable since I drank a half a bottle of Benadryl and slept through most of it. Stumbling through the Marseilles airport wasn't too bad either since I was groggy and hung over from the Benadryl. Plus it made the time less noticeable as I waited for the bus to take me to Aix-en-Provence which it turns out is *not* walking distance from Marseilles.

Anyway, I have to say France would not have been my first choice for a fun trip but Gilbert had done a college internship or something there years ago and was always raving about how great it was. The food, the weather, the scenery, blah blah blah.

So when the house swap opportunity popped up in my email it seemed like another sign that our relationship was going in the right direction. The gods were smiling. Right up until now when they were totally busting a gut laughing.

Anyway without too much misdirection and misunderstanding I eventually ended up on the right bus which took me to Aix and from there I fell into a taxi which succeeded in taking me to the address of the apartment building that I'd traded my natty Buckhead condo for on what, again, was supposed to have been walking distance from Aix.

Uh, no.

As I watched the lights of Aix disappear behind me in the rear window of the taxi, I realized somebody had made a very big mistake and naturally that somebody was me.

The village of Chabanel where I'd unwittingly swapped my condo was at least ten miles outside the Aix city limits. Later, perfectly reasonable people would explain to me that Chabanel was technically considered a part of what was called the "commune" of Aix and ergo the misunderstanding.

In any case, I'm not sure what I was expecting but I already had a bad feeling by the time the driver stopped and deposited my bags on the cobblestone street in front of an ominous wall of ancient ornately carved wooden doors in a village the size of a strip mall parking lot.

My first thought was that the taxi driver had taken me someplace where his nefarious accomplices could mug me because there was no way *this* place could be where I was staying.

From what I could see I'd been landed in a backlot movie set for a medieval village. The street was so narrow I could literally reach out and touch the buildings on either side of it. The windows were dark and shuttered.

The words *creepy* and *inhospitable* came to mind. It was impossible to imagine there was an apartment inside this building that *didn't* have a dead body hanging in the closet or a selection of hooks and bloody chains in the basement.

The Poupards—whose apartment I had swapped for my gorgeous little Atlanta condo—had texted me in the taxi to gush about the fact that they were happily ensconced in my home off Peachtree Road. They even sent a photo of the two of them grinning away in my flat and hoisting my own champagne glasses with my cat Hamish curled up between them.

In a normal world I would never have been able to afford such a great condo and in such a great area of town but my paternal grandfather had died a few years ago and left me just enough to cover the down payment. I was never close to Granddad Hooker and personally I always thought the gift was guilt money for saddling me with such a crap last name.

My condo had been furnished to replicate how I imagined Dorothy Parker might have lived if Dorothy Parker had lived in Atlanta in 2017. I had an insanely expensive Chesterfield leather sofa anchoring my living room and matched with Pottery Barn side tables, a 52" flat screen, and two paintings that cost me a month's salary each.

Not that the money was the important thing, but honestly, a month's salary!

The minute I looked up at the façade of the apartment building that was to be my home and refuge for the next two weeks in France, I was sure I was going to have to find a hotel instead. Except there were no hotels that I could see and anyway I didn't have enough money for a room and also eat for the next two weeks.

My next inclination was to burst into tears but honestly I'd done a good deal of that in the weeks since Gilbert gave me his *let's go our own way and maybe we'll find our way back to each other* speech and frankly it never made me feel one bit better.

My girlfriend, CeCe subscribed to the old *time heals all wounds* theory which I was sick of hearing by the time I left.

I needed relief from this agony *now*—not a year from now or whenever the adage had me lined up for feeling normal again.

In any case, I trudged up the narrow winding staircase, dragging my carry-on behind me. Every step reminded me of why I had gotten the bad end of the stick in this debacle.

The marble stairs inside the apartment building were so slick and shiny from centuries of people walking up and down them—probably since Roman times—that I clutched the handrail for fear of plunging to my death down the stairwell as I thought about the Poupards who had a nice modern elevator with carpeted everything to cushion their journey from parking lot to condo.

It wasn't fair. I was pretty sure Sabine and Jacques Poupard hadn't accurately represented the apartment in the online photos and when I put the key they'd mailed me in the door and opened it up, I could see I was right.

※ ※ ※ ※ ※ ※

Two hours after opening the door to the Poupard's apartment and a scant hour after indulging in another cathartic but basically useless crying jag, I'd discovered that an engineering degree was required to operate the unbelievably small washing machine in the tiny kitchen and that there was, in fact, no dryer and no dishwasher to be found at all unless you counted me.

The kitchen, dining room and living room were all rolled into one room that couldn't be more than a dozen feet long or wide. The bedroom was even smaller with the double bed and tiny bedside table just barely fitting.

The Poupards must be midgets, I decided. Either that or they don't both live here at the same time. It was impossible to believe this was to be my home for the next two weeks.

Exhausted and downhearted, I didn't bother to unpack but opened my suitcase where I'd dropped it on the living room floor and pulled out my slippers. It was June and what that meant in Atlanta was gorgeous flowers and sky-high air conditioning bills.

Obviously what it meant in Chabanel was gorgeous flowers and no air conditioning at all. I wiped a sheen of sweat from my top lip.

I had to admit the view from the third floor was pretty nice. It wasn't the Mediterranean; we were too far inland for that, but it did afford a nice view of orange tile rooftops. If you squinted you could erase all the television antennas that sprouted from all the roofs and the scene was quite pretty.

Checking my watch to see what time it was in Atlanta, I put in a quick call to my best friend CeCe.

CeCe worked with me at the Atlanta Journal Constitution. We were both reporters, had both graduated at the top of our respective journalism school classes and both were in the process of slogging away most of our youth writing wedding announcements, obits and the odd movie review. It wasn't great plus it paid crap because the whole world had decided that they didn't really need a newspaper any more.

Hey, I feel the same way! I get my news online too, but still! What about all those poor over-educated people trying to support themselves in a dying profession?

People can be so selfish.

"Jules!" CeCe said with as much enthusiasm as a four a.m. phone call on her end would allow. "You're in France! How is it?"

"It sucks," I said, knowing I sounded like a brat but since I'd recently had my heart broken I'd learned I could get away with a whole range of new and unattractive behavior I wouldn't normally be able to.

"Oh, I'm sorry. What's bad about it?"

"For starters, the apartment is a dump," I said. "It's prehistoric. I'm not even kidding."

"Well, you know things in France are a lot older than in the US."

"There's no microwave, no dishwasher, no dryer, no garbage disposal and only two burners on the stove!"

"Well, you don't really cook much, do you?"

"That is not the point, CeCe." I could feel the exhaustion of the day translate into pique as my best friend stubbornly refused to see how awful my life was at the moment.

"I know, hon, but France has so many amazing things that it would be a shame not to enjoy them while you're there. Like the amazing food and the baked goods. Have you looked around the neighborhood?"

"I'm afraid to! And that reminds me. I need you to run by my condo and check on the Poupards. Now that I see where they live in France, it's pretty clear they're criminal low-life types."

"You crack me up, Jules," CeCe said with a laugh. "Have you met any of your neighbors?"

"No. Did you forget I don't speak French?"

"A smile translates in any language."

"Excuse the long pause. I had to throw up a little."

"Jules, I'm just going to tell you that you're in paradise and that you really don't want to be back here right now. You really don't."

"Have you seen Gilbert?" I sat up straight as the thought came to me. I had met Gilbert through CeCe. There was every reason to think she might have recently bumped into him.

"I haven't," CeCe said tiredly. "And I really hope you do yourself a favor and try to put him out of your mind while you're over there."

I gnawed on a fingernail and thought I saw something moving on the floor in the kitchen. I stood up to inch my way in there, holding my breath that it wasn't a roach or, worse, a rat.

"Promise me, Jules? Promise me you'll focus on being there, and be open to the experiences you'll have, the people you'll meet?"

I edged my way into the small alcove of a kitchen and jumped back with a yelp when I saw that a small black cat had materialized on the kitchen rug.

"What happened?"

"There's a cat here!"

"Well, you have a cat at your place too."

"Yes, but mine was part of the deal. They never mentioned anything about having a cat."

The cat cocked its head as if to get a better look at me and I had the distinct impression it was giving me the once over.

"Okay, Jules," CeCe said with a yawn. "I need to be up and at 'em in about two hours so I will leave you now."

I squatted and as soon as I did the cat ran to me and rubbed its face on my knee. I put a hand out to pet it and it twisted around and tried to bite me. I pulled my hand away and it hissed at me.

"Making friends, it sounds like?"

"Yeah, so much," I said as I watched the cat jump on the kitchen counter and walk over to the stove.

"Jules?"

"Yes, yes, go back to sleep," I said, feeling the exhaustion cascade over me as I said the words. I had yet to check out the bedroom and was relieved to realize that I was too tired to care what it was like.

"Promise me you'll try to accept where you are right now, Jules?"

"Yes, of course."

"I'm serious. The sooner you do, the happier you'll be."

"Remind me to embroider that on a pillow."

"I'll text you later, sweetie."

I disconnected and tossed my phone into my open suitcase, then took three steps to the bedroom and sank down on the bed without another thought about where I was or what I'd gotten myself into.

2

The Slow Everything Movement

I slept the rest of the day and all night long, waking just before nine the next morning. I'm not sure it was the noise or the light that woke me.

The noise had to do with the discordant screeching of two fishwives somewhere below my window which was open and which must have been open even before I arrived because I certainly hadn't opened it. And the light had to do with the fact that the sun was glaring into my bedroom.

I staggered to the window to pull the blinds shut and then to the bathroom and finally to the kitchen. I was overjoyed to see the Poupards had left me, among other things, a jug of freshly squeezed orange juice.

I'd left them a bottle of champagne, a basket of Georgia peaches and a box of chocolates.

The orange juice was probably the most delicious thing I'd ever tasted but some of that had to do with the fact that I was both dehydrated and starving.

I tried to imagine Gilbert sleeping in this bed with me. After all, I'd picked this place out on the Internet thinking he would be with me.

Somehow the image wouldn't gel. I glanced at my phone to see if he'd answered any of the texts I'd sent him yesterday but there was nothing.

After showering and changing into shorts and a cotton blouse with sandals, I locked the apartment and made my way very carefully down the slick stairs to the main floor. I had to admit the building looked much less threatening in the morning. In fact now that I got a good look at it I could see there were window boxes of bright red geraniums in most of the windows.

Plus, I have to say that the bathroom did not suck. It was very modern and even somewhat spacious. It didn't quite make up for the tiny kitchen and the lack of basic kitchen appliances but it helped.

I plugged in the words *Cours Mirabeau* into my phone's GPS since I'd researched that it was the main shopping district in Aix and then watched as my screen formed an easy-to-follow map. Ten miles away.

I'm usually very good at researching projects and so I instantly kicked myself for not knowing that my new digs were so far away from the city of Aix. What the heck was I going to do in a podunk village circa 1100 A.D.? And how was I going to get to Aix? When the taxi driver drove me through the dinky main street of Chabanel I couldn't help but notice that there was no bus station and no taxi stands.

I stood for a moment on the street where my apartment building was located and noted that the street sign—a blue metal sculpted placard with white letters—read *rue Gaston de Saporta*. It didn't really flow off the tongue but I didn't expect to need to ever remember it after this visit.

The street headed south in the direction that the taxi had come from. The note in the kitchen that the Poupards had left me said there were two bakeries in the village and several nice restaurants. I knew by now of course that the Poupards were incorrigible liars but I still intended to see for myself.

As I walked I passed a few women with children who looked at me with suspicion and the closer I got to what had to be the center of the village, the more people I saw. I noticed that nobody was drinking coffee as they walked. That's something you'd see in any normal city in America,

I thought. But for some reason people here wanted to sit down to drink their coffee.

After passing the first bakery I came to I decided to go ahead and get a breakfast bun since I wasn't sure if any of the restaurants were open and serving yet.

The next bakery was small with a large display window crowded with about a jillion glossy tarts and pies, cookies, and cream-filled pastries. I usually got the almond croissant at my local Starbucks in Atlanta so I thought that would be a safe choice here.

The bell jangled merrily as I entered and the proprietor —a heavyset woman in her late forties—turned to look at me.

"*Bonjour*!" she sang out, but her face was unsmiling.

"*Bonjour*," I said approaching the counter. There was nobody else in the bakery and I wasn't sure whether that was a sign that I was shopping for breakfast later than most people did or that it meant this bakery was no good.

It really didn't matter. As long as the croissant didn't give me food poisoning, I didn't care.

"Uh, *une* of those, *s'il vous plait*," I said, pointing to a croissant.

She bagged it up and spouted off something very fast in French which presumably was the amount of money she wanted from me. I handed her a five euro note and she made change and handed me the bag.

In and out in under two minutes and only moderately stressful.

Except it wasn't an almond croissant in my bag. And I'm pretty sure it shouldn't have cost four euros ten.

Oh, well. I went to the nearest bench on the street and sat and ate the croissant. I would've loved to have had it with a cup of coffee but obviously people do things one at a time over here.

Another reason to get on the next airplane back to Atlanta.

Until the words had formed in my head, I hadn't realized that I was, in fact, thinking of leaving. But once I realized it, well, it was all I could do not to call American Airlines right then and get my return flight moved up.

Unfortunately, for whatever reason, Internet connection was dodgy on this particular street so I'd have to wait until I was back at the apartment to call the airline.

But just the thought of returning home put an extra bounce in my step that hadn't been there before. I figured I could take a breath and wait a day to make it happen.

I finished off the croissant and had to admit that—although not almond—it was still exquisitely delicious. In fact, it beat the Starbucks almond croissant all to hell and back. There was a buttery flakiness that was hard to describe. It just melted in my mouth in a kind of perfect harmony of sugar-meets-perfection.

Now that I thought about it, it had totally been worth four euros ten.

I continued my trek to the center of the village and now that I'd had something to eat, I felt much better. A handsome young Arab-type guy passed me on the street and while it was true he raked me from chest to feet with his eyes, he did get eye contact with me and he did smile.

It was nice to know I hadn't totally fallen off the radar of a handsome guy.

The sun splintered across the tall buildings that bordered the narrow alleys and felt warm on my back. This section of Chabanel was obviously a pedestrian-only area and I felt myself relaxing as I slowed my pace to look into shop windows and made my way to the heart of the village.

There in the middle of a roundabout was a monument to war dead from both world wars. There was a profuse planting of flowers at the base which was certainly the prettiest thing I'd seen in the village so far and showed me what the good people of Chabanel thought about their veterans. Facing the monument was a large cream-colored building with a big clock on the front and what looked like air raid horns on the roof.

Across from that was something called *Casino* which looked more like a grocery store than any place you might want to place a bet. And then there was a charming golden building with forest green shutters with the words *Police Municipale* on it and the French flag waving gaily on both sides of the massive wooden double doors.

I walked on until I saw more and more people, most of them walking with bags of baked goods and fresh produce. I decided to follow the crowd.

❊❊❊❊❊

Luc DeBray stood at the window of his office and stared out at the street below. He'd been at the station since before seven and was already looking forward to his lunch which he anticipated enjoying alone at Café Sucre.

He knew the proprietor there, Theo Bardot, and because Luc was who he was he knew he could always count on special service

Not that it mattered. The food at Café Sucre was always good and it didn't matter if you were the Chief of the Chabanel *Police Municipale* or a hapless tourist bound to mispronounce every item on the menu.

Luc sighed and turned away from the window. His sergeant Eloise Basile came in with a raised eyebrow but he waved her away. It was not unusual any time of year to be having such a spate of peace and quiet. Unlike Aix which was rife with the usual problems of any tourist town especially during the summer, the typical Chabanel crime wave was mostly drunks, the occasional domestic disturbance and a few complaints from British or German tourists. The Americans rarely strayed from Aix.

Not that Chabanel didn't have its share of violence, but nothing to compare with Aix or for that matter any American city of similar size.

He glanced at his computer screen and glimpsed a crime report coming in from Nice. Now *that* was a city with real crime and real problems, he thought. Murders in Nice rolled in every few nights, not just once every six months as in Aix.

No, Luc did not envy the police force there who most certainly were not spending any part of their morning contemplating where they might have lunch today.

Not for the first time Luc found himself wishing France had CCTV cameras on every street corner. He was sure that fact had less to do with violating civil liberties, than it did spoiling the view of a twelfth century village for the paying customers.

With an annoyed grunt, he sat back down at his desk to see if there was anything in the report that might impact Chabanel or, God forbid, his lunch.

3

Easy Come, Easy Go

Well, at least my trip to the produce market didn't totally suck.

It was actually kind of fun. I mean, I wasn't singing in the streets a la Maria von Trapp but I have to admit there was something about the hustle of the crowd picking through the vast assortment of produce—all so beautifully arranged—that was a definite pick-me-up.

I smelled the sweet fragrance of lavender before I'd even turned the corner and saw table after table groaning with bulging hemp bags of lavender seeds and flowers, each bag with little signs jammed into the middle indicating the price.

And then there were the olives!

Oh. My. God.

Barrels of them, glistening and bobbing in olive oil and flecked with God knows what herbs and spices. I'd never seen so many colors. Purple. Black. At least four different shades of green. Blue, I swear I saw blue olives.

I bought more than I could eat in a week—let alone a day because by now I'd pretty much decided that, pretty farmers' market or not, I was leaving as soon as I could get a flight out.

I wove my way into the thick of where most of the people were obviously stocking up for a major feast, and I bought a basket to carry all the stuff I intended to buy. One table was loaded with fresh sausages, another with row after row of apricots and strawberries. I bought little baskets of each. The flowers were everywhere—not just lavender but sunflowers—some as big as my head—and freesias and roses and tulips.

There was even a stand selling bread—glossy ropes of braided bread, brioche, olive bread and of course the ubiquitous croissants. For some reason I bought enough to feed half the apartment building.

As I was walking through the market I swear I could feel the vibe of all these different people—most of whom probably shopped here every day or however often the market was held. It was fun to get lost in the crowd of people who were so intent on shopping and doing their thing. It was like being in a big wave that just carried you along.

I never tend to let myself give up control for long and for the mere moments that I did allow it at the market, well, it was very nice.

As I turned a corner, revealing another long row of produce stands, I saw a man who was staring at me. It was so strange because it was almost as if he'd been waiting for me or knew I was about to come around the corner—although that was impossible—but I have to say it totally creeped me out.

But the discomfort didn't last because right about then I discovered the cheese kiosk.

Honestly I think I just stood and stared for at least a minute and the woman manning the cheese stand didn't seem at all concerned or surprised about that so I guess it happens a lot.

The woman behind the table waved me over, breaking the spell.

"My French no being good," I said, hoping my winning smile would take the sting out of my absent language skills.

"American?" she asked with a friendly smile.

I nodded and looked at her wares. The larger wheels of cheese, smooth as plastic, were wedged behind the front rows of smaller packages of cheese wrapped in leaves and waxed paper and held together with twine.

"This is amazing," I said. "*Le* amazing." I cringed when that slipped out like I thought that slapping a *le* onto an English word would turn it into a French word. But she either didn't notice or had heard worse from other tourists.

"You are liking cheese?" she said as she grabbed a small knife and a chunk of bread. Within seconds she'd slathered a rich and gooey cheesy concoction on the bread and handed it to me.

As I eagerly took it from her, I now realized that the almond croissant, as good as it was, hadn't taken much of a dent out of my hunger.

At the first bite I have to say the flavor was so intense I closed my eyes to relish the experience. The cheese melted on my tongue and the flavor was so full and so different from anything I'd ever had before, a part of me felt like I was dreaming.

"My God," I said, finally opening my eyes.

I knew that if I bought too much cheese it would just rot in my little apartment fridge but I bought a ton of it anyway. Mini-wheels of Comte and gooey cartons of Morbier and Camembert, plus some of the sample I'd had which turned out to be something called *bleu d'Auvergne*.

The cheese lady—who looked to be around my own age—introduced herself as Katrine Pelletier. She had a wide smile and blue eyes that crinkled when she laughed. She was the total antithesis of the cold French person I'd always heard about.

After I paid for my cheese purchases said goodbye and continued on my way. I actually found myself feeling sorry for the fact that I'd never see her again.

❄❄❄❄❄

I had barely put my market basket down in my apartment before I was at my computer changing my return flight. I'd already figured I could stay at a Holiday Inn in Buckhead until the Poupards left my apartment—unless I could convince them to take the Holiday Inn instead. I paid a significant penalty to make the return flight change but it was worth it.

Not that my little market jaunt hadn't been pleasant—but it was even more pleasant as soon as I knew I was leaving. After I changed the flight, I opened an email from Jenna Zimmerman, my boss.

She'd been with the paper for decades and I wasn't entirely sure she liked me but the subject line read: *Keep this under your hat* which was way too playful for Jenna and way too intriguing for me not to read it immediately.

Although definitely veiled, it seemed Jenna was suggesting that I'd be up for a promotion when I got back.

A promotion. That meant a regular column. It was the one thing I'd been working toward for the past four years. It was the reason I'd given up a stringer position on a smaller paper in Florida—because I thought I might have a chance to be a real reporter in Atlanta.

I reread the email and confirmed that that was indeed what Jenna was hinting at.

And then I sat back and wondered why I wasn't bouncing off the walls with glee.

This was the thing I'd been waiting for! I'd worked for it! I'd earned it! It was happening!

Why didn't I care?

I stared at the email and decided that the reason for my lack of euphoria had to be the emotional hangover of my breakup with Gilbert. For this to finally be happening for me and for me *not* to be over the moon about it had to mean that my heartache was coloring every part of my life.

Nothing is good right now. Even the croissants don't taste amazing. Well, actually they do. But everything else in life was just less than it could be.

I was tempted to send an email to CeCe to see if she'd gotten a similar email from Jenna but decided to wait for her to say something first.

I closed my laptop and felt—I can't say *better*—but at least resolved that I had a plan and that plan didn't involve sitting in a crappy medieval apartment eating apricots for two weeks while Gilbert went on a dating spree in Atlanta.

I was going back to Atlanta—to a new position of respect and esteem. This news literally could not have come at a better time, I told myself.

I went to the tiny kitchen and unpacked the market goodies that I'd bought and spent a few moments washing strawberries and imagining Gilbert's face when I bumped into him on the street after I won the Pulitzer for Investigative News Reporting .

"Jules! I read about your towering achievement and all I can say is wow! Congratulations! Are you free tonight?"

"Gilbert, you said? I'm sorry. I'm trying to place you..."

That made me feel better for a moment and then I ate two of the chocolate brioches and that helped quite a bit too.

Just as I was trying to figure out how to turn on the gas stove to see if I could make a cup of tea, there was a knock on the door. I frowned because while I'd decided that the apartment building didn't actually seem to be anchoring a slum, neither was I looking forward to a complicated exchange with real live French people on some matter that I'm pretty sure had nothing to do with me.

I turned the gas off and went to the door.

Just as I feared, I opened the door to find three women who were all talking at once in French. Two of the women were quite elderly and resembled each other and spoke rapid, incomprehensible French, but the other woman—who looked to be in her mid-twenties—smiled apologetically.

"You are the American, yes?" the girl said.

"Yes, *bonjour*," I said. It was late afternoon and so that probably wasn't right but I wasn't going to sweat it. In about fifteen hours I need never worry again about whether it was *bonjour* or *bon soir* or *bon* what the hell.

"I am Merci Joslin. I am living two doors down, *oui*?" She motioned with her head in the direction of where her apartment was. The old ladies clucked and fluttered their hands.

"Okay. Good to know," I said, glancing at the two elderly aunties with her.

"This is Madame Becque and Madame Cazaly," Merci said, indicating the old ladies. "They have a problem and I cannot help them. I have to go to work."

Well, hell's bells, I can't help them! I wanted to say, but already the old ladies—who I could see now were twins—were peering into my apartment as if the answer to their problem was somehow inside.

"They are losing their...*petite chat*, yes? You are knowing this?"

"I have no—"

"Meow! Meow!" Merci said as the two elderly Madame twins began to nod their heads.

"Lost their cat, got it," I said. "Oh! Is it black? And evil? Because I might know where it is."

"Not black, *non*," Merci said. "White, I think. But I must go. *Je suis désolé.*"

She patted the arm of the one of the old ladies and looked at me with a shrug. "So sorry." And then she hurried down the hall to the stairwell.

I looked back at Madames Becque and Cazaly as they pushed their way into my apartment.

"Uh, yeah, okay, please come in," I said as I followed them. Madame Becque went instantly to my stove and put the kettle on while Madame Cazaly strode to the balcony and began calling to her cat in sing-songy French.

I stood in the tiny living room not at all sure what to do next when Madame Cazaly hurried back to me and began speaking quickly as she wrung her hands.

Okay, this isn't working at all, I thought.

Both ladies had to be in their nineties. It was a miracle to me that they could get around they way they did. They didn't seem to limp or to walk particularly slowly at all. Maybe if you walked over lumpy cobblestones all your life your joints just kept lubricated or something. But agile or not, it still didn't change the fact that I did not understand a word of what they were saying.

"*Thé, Madame?*" Madame Becque called to me from the kitchen. "*Ou café?*"

"Uh, tea?" I said uncertainly.

Her sister—because by now it was dead clear they were at least sisters—began gesticulating as if she had an idea of what I should be doing.

"Go downstairs?" I said. "Are you saying you want me to look for the cat downstairs?"

She just made the same useless hand gestures she'd made before.

I felt a wave of frustration. Thank God I wouldn't have to deal with this after tomorrow!

"What is the cat's name?" I asked.

She looked at me and frowned in incomprehension.

I mimicked calling to a cat. "Come, Princess. Where are you...Fluffy? Here, Puss! Kitty-kitty-kitty?"

The sister in the kitchen spoke sharply to Madame Cazaly—the twin I could already tell was the shy one—who nodded vigorously.

"*Oui, Camille!*" Madame Cazaly said, and her eyes filled with tears.

"Okay," I said. "The cat's name is Camille. Okay. You stay here." I motioned for her to stay in the living room. "Me go to street. Me look."

I didn't think she understood a word of what I said but she nodded and her eyes looked so hopeful and almost happy that I knew I had to at least try to find the damn cat.

"I'll be right back," I said uselessly and then hurried out the apartment down the hall and down the slippery stairwell.

I couldn't believe I was going to spend my last evening in France rooting around a neighborhood I didn't know trying to find a lost cat who was probably feral as hell and would give me cat scratch fever as a parting souvenir of my trip. But I also knew I couldn't at least try.

When I got to the street I saw the sun had dropped nearer the horizon. Being June, I knew I had plenty of daylight left but it was late afternoon. I stood on the street and took my bearings. There were only about a million places a cat might hide.

My own cat back in Atlanta often opened the kitchen cupboards and curled up among the pots and pans for some reason understandable only to him. I assumed that the Madame sisters had checked their own apartment pretty thoroughly before enlisting my help. If not, then I imagined that little chore was ahead on my night's agenda.

The street was quiet with only pedestrians but even though the taxi had dropped me off here the day before, it hardly seemed wide enough to accommodate vehicles.

I scanned the street on both sides, trying to see if there was a cat perhaps on the ledge or atop the windows boxes across from my own building. But there was nothing. At least nothing that I could see. The stupid cat might very well be watching me at this very moment and I'd never know it.

Then it occurred to me that the first thing Madame C had done was go to my balcony and look out. Maybe she thought the kitty was down there? My balcony was on the far side of the building and looked over a seriously overgrown garden bordered by a tractor road that probably led to a nearby field.

At least it was some place to look. I hurried down the street until I rounded the corner of my apartment building and entered a dark narrow alley between my building and the one behind it.

Careful not to touch the dirty walls, I hurried down the alley until I came out the other end behind my building.

The garden must have been quite something in its day. I know very little about flowers or back yards as I live in a condo in a big city and am happy not to have to worry about lawns or flower beds. But even I could see that this back patch had once been loved and carefully tended.

The cascading bougainvillea was growing wild now and many other overgrown flowering shrubs lined the perimeter of the little courtyard. I knew that, unlike the English, the French preferred orderly and tidy gardens. But this back garden was definitely wild and free.

As I looked at the tangled twisting wisteria vines snaking down the backside of the apartment building and the profusion of wild rose bushes, I thought even the English would probably say this was a bit much.

There must be nearly a million places a cat could hide in all this.

Why hadn't I thought to bring something down with me to entice it with? I should have asked Madame C for some kitty kibble or even a can of tuna.

Except my French is so bad I couldn't ask her to pour water on me if I were on fire.

"Camille?" I sang. "Kitty-kitty-kitty?"

I assumed that kitty-kitty was the universal language of all cats although that's probably terribly obnoxiously American of me.

I swear to you I was so convinced that this was the wildest of wild goose chases that only one other thing that happened that afternoon shocked me more as abruptly as hearing a faint answering meow coming from the midst of that bramble of rose bushes.

But that other thing was probably the biggest shock of my life.

In my excitement to see if I'd really and truly found the elusive Camille, and stupidly ignoring the fact that there were probably dozens of venomous snakes all through the brush—*what kind of a Georgia girl are you anyway?*—I plunged into the tall stand of bushes, feeling the thorny branches scrape against my bare legs in my eagerness to catch any sign of the white kitty I was now convinced was there.

And of course she was. I could see her big green curious eyes as she watched me approach.

I saw her only a split second before I glanced down and saw what she was sitting beside.

Sticking straight out of the ground before me was a human arm.

4

When You Least Expect It

I couldn't breathe.

I'll tell you that right now.

I looked at that arm sticking out of the ground and I felt my breath just leave my lungs in one painful whoosh. I remember staggering backwards into an ancient rose bush and the feeling of those thorns jabbing into my shins pulled me out of whatever catatonic state I feel pretty sure I was about to degenerate into.

As soon as I was no longer looking at the ...thing, I felt better. And as soon as I was able to turn and run out of the garden and down the alley, I felt better still. But if you'd run into me then, you probably wouldn't believe it because as soon as I hit the street I started gasping and screaming.

I looked around wildly for anyone who might help me —or hell, understand me. And then I remembered that I had my cellphone in my shorts pocket. I stood on the corner, my hands shaking, and dialed 112—which I had read on the flight over was the thing to do in case of an emergency. And I cannot tell you how many times I looked over my shoulder to make sure that arm was not going to come up out of the ground after me.

Talk about losing your mind.

I would be totally crap at any kind of job that really mattered, like being a cop or a solider or a nurse. I would just go to pieces, well, much like I did when I stood on the corner hyperventilating and trying to jab in the right numbers on my phone.

When the dispatcher picked up I knew there would be the whole language issue but this was so close to Aix—a major tourist town—and I guessed the cops weren't totally unused to foreigners calling with their problems.

"I...I've found a body," I blurted out as soon as the dispatcher picked up.

"Your name, Madame?'

"Julia Hooker," I said. "I'm staying at..." And naturally my mind went blank. You'd never know I was an investigative reporter—or at least aspired to be an investigative reporter. I literally had to run to the end of the street and look up at the blue ceramic street sign to tell the woman what road I lived on.

"You will stay there?" she asked me except it didn't really sound like a request.

"I will, yes," I said. I hung up and hugged the phone to my chest. I felt better. Someone else—someone who was accustomed to dealing with this sort of thing would take over now. I swallowed and leaned against the rough limestone wall of the building.

I smelled him before I saw him.

"*Ça va?*" a deep male voice said to me from behind. I whirled around to face a tall man dressed in a t-shirt and baggy jeans. His face was haggard and lined and his long hair was down to his shoulders. He was the man I'd seen earlier in the market who'd been watching me. I hope I didn't actually recoil when he stepped up to me but I think by the look on his face that I must have.

"I...I don't speak French," I said. I didn't even have the presence of mind to say it in French and that was one of the few phrases I actually knew.

Had he followed me home from the market?

He looked in the direction of the alley I'd just come from and asked me something else I didn't understand.

"I just found a dead body," I said, knowing he wouldn't understand me but it felt good to say it out loud. "It totally freaked me out. Buried in the back garden."

He frowned and looked back at the alley.

For a minute I thought he might go into the alley and I wasn't at all sure that was a good idea. Right then I heard the sound of the melodic police siren you only hear in France.

Thank God, I thought and the relief coursed through me.

That poor girl. It surprised me to realize that I was thinking that the arm belonged to a woman since I'd only seen it so briefly before I panicked and bolted, but my mind had seared the image into my brain. It hadn't been a masculine arm.

My knees felt like they were about to give out and I leaned hard against the wall. As I watched the police car pull into the street, I turned around and noticed that the creepy man who'd spoken to me had disappeared.

❊❊❊❊❊

The police car parked right in front of me. Two policemen with serious faces got out, one fat and one elderly and neither of whom spoke English. I pointed to the alley and said "Down there," and was grateful they didn't require me to lead them in.

They disappeared into the alley as another police car arrived. This time there was a woman gendarme and a guy who was obviously the boss. Once out of the car, he said something into a communicator on his collar while glancing over at me.

Before going into the alley, he spoke briefly to the woman, who then walked over to me.

I'm not sure what the point of that was since she didn't speak English but probably it was to keep me from walking off which now that the cops were here I was thinking was exactly what I wanted to do.

She flipped out a notepad like she was going to ask me questions but I think it was really just to demonstrate to me that I needed to stay put. I tried to smile at her or connect with her in someway but she didn't respond. I can't blame her really. She couldn't talk to me so what was the point of pantomiming pleasantness?

After all, I'd seen enough detective TV shows to know that until proven otherwise the one who finds the body is the first suspect.

We waited in silence, my heart pounding in my throat as I tried to remember exactly what it was that I'd seen. Was it possible it *wasn't* a dead body? Could I have overreacted? Been mistaken?

I think a part of me had half convinced myself that I was going to be terribly embarrassed when the cops came out of the alleyway saying I'd only seen a harmless cemetery for plastic store manikins. Maybe that was something the French might do in deference to their obsessive affinity for the fashion industry.

So when the good-looking boss cop came out of the alley—and it startled me to realize I'd registered that he was good-looking—I was shocked all over again to see that he was definitely not treating this as a joke or a mistake.

His expression was grim as he walked over to me. Grim like he'd just seen a dead body.

He spoke rapidly to the Sergeant Girl Friday, who then went to the police car and pulled out a wheel of crime scene tape.

"I am Chief Luc DeBray, head of the *police municipale* in Chabanel" the guy said to me, his eyes appraising me openly. "You are Madame Hooker?"

Wow. I'd never heard that combination of my name before and I have to say I hate it worse than anything else I've ever heard with it before. It's true that *hooker* isn't the ugly word it used to be in the fifties now that *ho* has taken over so much of its work, but it's still an effective trigger for the butt of many a lewd joke. And trust me I know.

It dawned on me right there standing on a side street in a tiny Provençal village in France that getting rid of my last name might have been at least part of the reason why I'd been so desperate to marry Gilbert.

"Yes," I said. "I'm Julia Hooker. Thank God you speak English."

He looked over his shoulder as the female cop was sealing off the entrance to the alley and speaking to a few of the neighbors who'd gathered to ask questions. He took my arm—shocking me again since I don't think American cops are supposed to touch you but I may be wrong about that—and led me firmly down the street.

Just when I was sure he was going to put me in the back of the squad car and read me my rights, we walked past the car to the end of the street.

Amazingly, he walked me to an outdoor café that I hadn't noticed that morning when I'd left the apartment. It was small—only three tables were out on the sidewalk. We sat down and he ordered two coffees.

When the waiter left, DeBray turned to me and seemed to take me in. It was about now that I began to feel a little awkward in my shorts and sandals, although heavens, I knew there was a topless beach not thirty miles from where we were sitting.

"Can you tell me what happened?" he asked. His eyes were molten brown with pupils so dark you couldn't see them. His hair was dark too and he had full lips.

Okay. He was handsome. Really handsome. And I didn't see a wedding ring.

What was the matter with me? I must be in shock or something.

I could see he was waiting for me to answer his question and when I reran the tapes of what that question was I found myself wondering if he was asking me if I knew what had happened to the girl.

Did he think I did it?

"I...I have no idea," I said.

"Why were you in the garden? It is not where a visitor might go. It is off the beaten road, yes?"

"I was trying to find my neighbor's cat. Camille."

Stupid! He doesn't need to know the cat's name!

The waiter brought two tiny cups and saucers and a little glass pitcher full of an amber fluid. I realized with surprise that the detective had ordered brandy to go with the coffees.

Go France! I thought as I watched him pour a healthy dollop into my cup and hand it to me. Instantly I felt ashamed, first for feeling attracted to this French stranger and second for feeling any kind of delight at all about the brandy when that poor girl back there in the garden would never feel anything ever again.

"Do...do you know who she is?" I asked as I nearly drained my entire coffee cup in one swallow.

"Not yet," he said. "Your apartment belongs to Monsieur and Madame Poupard, *n'est-ce pas*?"

"Yes, we house swapped," I said. *Surely he didn't think I'd do a house swap so I could kill some random girl in France?*

"And you arrived yesterday?"

Wow. Had he already found this out? How? Had he talked to the Madame sisters? Or called Sabine and Jacques Poupard? The taxi driver? How did he know this?

"Yes," I said, feeling the warming effects of the brandy in my veins and wondering if that was all a part of his plan. "Yesterday."

He raised an eyebrow and waited as if expecting me to say more.

Oh, crap! He thinks I killed her! Instantly my stomach gave an unpleasant lurch. I noticed my fingers on my coffee cup were trembling and I quickly put them in my lap so he wouldn't see. *I must look the picture of the guilty party*, I thought, and then had a terrible thought. *Will this prevent me from leaving tomorrow as planned?*

Suddenly the light in the street seemed to glow very bright and then flash. Several of the people in the café gasped so I assumed it wasn't something that happened every day around here. The detective was frowning and watching the horizon when the waiter came back out and spoke to him.

DeBray cursed in French and stood up.

"You will stay here, yes?" he said but just like the female cop, he didn't wait to hear my answer. He followed the waiter back inside the café.

The rest of the café patrons were talking excitedly to themselves but they weren't looking at me and after a moment one of them laughed and whatever had happened with the bright flash in the sky seemed to lose their interest.

Two cars were stopped in the street the café was facing. One was close by and its driver was outside the vehicle cursing loudly. It did seem very strange that both cars would stall out at the exact same time. My mind began to spin.

Why did the waiter need to talk to the police chief?

And why did DeBray jump up as if what the waiter told him was even more important than a dead body in the garden?

I watched the driver pound on the hood of his car in frustration and then throw his cellphone into the car before looking around at all of us watching him.

Something was wrong.

But what could be more wrong than murder?

5

The Other Shoe, She is Dropping

Luc stared at the bank of kitchen equipment—two ovens, several espresso makers, blenders, grills. The café owner Theo stared at him as if he were responsible for this *catastrophe*.

Nothing was working. No lights. Nothing.

"What is happening?" Theo asked in bewilderment.

"Has this never happened before?" Luc asked. But he knew before he asked the question that this was no normal blackout.

The two cars stalled in the middle of the road told him that.

"Never! We have battery-operated lights but they aren't working either."

Luc looked around the kitchen and felt a burning eagerness to get back to his crime scene. He checked his collar *communique* but he wasn't surprised to find it was dead too.

If the bright flash—combined with the nonworking electrical appliances and his dead communications device—meant what he feared it meant, he needed to get back to his team immediately.

"What should we do?" Theo asked.

"What can you still do? Coffee? Food?"

Theo looked around his kitchen and shrugged. "Perhaps not espresso, but we can serve cold food. And of course wine."

"*Bon*," Luc said as he turned away. "Do that until it gets dark and then close early."

"We will lose a fortune!"

But Luc was already on his way out.

❈❈❈❈❈

I think it was right about the time that the police chief walked past me without even looking at me that I figured I was probably free to go. Whatever had happened that had trumped his murder investigation—perhaps a stolen shipment of blueberry muffins?—at least it meant I appeared to be off the hook.

During the few moments when I wasn't noting how dishy he was I have to admit I'd spent a little bit of time obsessing about rotting away in a French prison while Gilbert was getting on with his life back in Atlanta. And while of course I didn't seriously begrudge CeCe taking my promotion, as she most assuredly would have in my place, I didn't love the idea either.

All in all, I was glad my portion of this drama was over and the whole event could now slink back into the realm of a really interesting travel story.

That was true for everyone, of course, except the poor woman in the garden.

Again, I have no idea how I knew the body was a woman's and it occurred to me that I should be relieved that I didn't blurt out that belief to Police Chief DeBray.

I finished my coffee and hurried back toward my neighborhood which now appeared to be remarkably full of people which I chalked up to the spreading of the news of the dead body. The first thing I saw when I turned down my street was that there was a car parked in the middle of the street alongside one of the cop cars and I had to admit that was bold even for the French. I'd already noted that they often drive on the sidewalk—and even park there too—but 'd yet to see one park in the street.

And alongside a cop car?

A niggling feeling began in the back of my mind. It was a feeling that said something didn't add up.

It was early evening now but still somewhat light out.

Even so, the streetlights should have been on.

Maybe that flash was a blown transformer?

That would be seriously annoying if it was. Life in a prehistoric apartment building was hard enough without having no electricity.

Two more cops were standing around the alley where the girl cop had draped her crime scene tape. I was surprised that the medical examiner hadn't shown up yet. I'd seen enough crime shows on TV. I knew the drill. First they protect the crime scene. Then the ME gives initial findings. Then the body is removed and the evidence is bagged.

Don't tell me they haven't removed the body yet? Things must really be old-fashioned here. Do they even *have* CSI teams?

I slowed my steps because by now it was clear that the lights were out on the street and in the buildings. And then I stopped and turned back, walking quickly in the direction I'd just come.

One thing living in Atlanta teaches you is how to deal with a power outage. Growing up there we had them at least weekly during the spring and for days at a time during the winter when we got our annual catastrophic one to two inches of snow. I knew what to do like I knew how to tie my shoes.

I'd seen what looked like a hardware shop across the street from the café that DeBray had taken me to and I remembered noticing that it was still open.

Sure enough, even without electricity the store was open for business. Although the cash register wasn't working, the proprietor had no problem totting up my order in his head and tucking my euros away in a drawer.

I bought two flashlights, a bag of batteries, another bag of candles and a small lantern—all of which I intended to leave as presents for the Poupards when I left—and hurried back to the street in front of my apartment. By the time I reached it I had to use one of the flashlights to find my way to the front door of the building.

With only the flashlight beams of the police crisscrossing up and down the street to see by, there were so many people milling about that it was like a block party.

It was then that I noticed that when you're in a crowd of people and you don't know their language, it's a lot like walking through a pleasant buzz of background noise. You can't understand their words so you don't get caught up in what they're saying and so your brain can turn off. Actually it's quite pleasant.

I made it up the darkened stairwell and shivered at how spooky and creepy it was. As soon as I got to my apartment door I paused for a total of ten seconds, debating whether to go to the old ladies' apartment and give them a report on the kitty hunt before deciding to give it a pass.

The door to my balcony was still open and from where I stood in the living room I could see a glow of light coming from the garden but I couldn't bring myself to look. If the body was still there, I definitely didn't want to look.

I set up the lantern and within moments. A soft light illuminated the room enough that I could see the food that I'd bought that afternoon. I unwrapped the bread and cheese along with the pears, grapes, berries and apricots, and laid out a sort of picnic for myself on the small coffee table in the sitting room. I went to the fridge—which was dark as I knew it would be—and pulled out the bottle of rosé that the Poupards has left for me. I poured myself a big glass before checking my laptop to see if there'd been any local news about the body yet.

I hadn't seen a reporter in all the commotion but if they were anything remotely like Atlanta, they got half their news listening to the police scanner.

My laptop was dead.

I have to say the first thing I felt when I realized my laptop wasn't working wasn't annoyance so much as apprehension. I'd fully charged my laptop before I went out today. There was no reason for it not to be working.

A part of my mind flashed back to the two motorists I'd seen beside their coincidentally stalled vehicles in the road. *Three* stalled vehicles if you counted the one in the street outside.

I wasn't sure what that meant but somehow I knew it was connected to my electronics not functioning. I found my cellphone where I'd put it on the counter when I came in.

It was dead too.

I sat there in front of my impromptu picnic looking at my dead cellphone and trying to fight down the burgeoning unease that was welling up in my chest when I heard a muffled noise outside my door that didn't make sense.

It was the sound of weeping.

6

The Big Bang

I opened my apartment door and somehow wasn't surprised to see the Madame Sisters standing in the hallway. Madame Cazaly—who I'd already pegged as the hysterical one—was the one crying. Her sister had an arm firmly around her shoulders and in the other hand held a dripping candle.

They looked at me as if it were D-Day and I was a part of the Allied forces here to save the day.

I have to say I was touched. Even if they were both crazy as loons.

I opened the door wider to usher them in and immediately Madame C stopped crying when she saw the glow of lights coming from inside my apartment.

"*Vous avez l'électricité!*" she blurted out in astonishment.

I don't know much French as must be evident by now but even I knew some words were the same in English as French.

"*Entrez, entrez,*" I said as I pulled them into the living room and settled them on the couch. The little picnic I'd set up almost looked as if I'd been expecting them. They must have thought so too because they regarded me with nothing less than amazement.

I quickly went to the kitchen to fetch two more wine glasses so as not to spoil the illusion. Once I'd poured their wine and handed out little plates for them to prepare their meals, I saw that they had begun to relax and I couldn't help but feel a wave of self-congratulation for the metamorphosis.

The door to the balcony was still open and the sounds and voices of the police working the crime scene below floated up. Again, I was saved the unfortunate chore of knowing *what* those voices were saying—something I suppose the Madame Sisters probably couldn't avoid.

"I am seeing Camille," I said in French, hoping to distract them from what they were hearing outside.

"Camille?" Madame C said as she held her wine glass halfway to her mouth.

"Today," I said. I decided it was best not to tell her precisely *where* I'd seen the cat so as not to totally wipe the look of jubilant expectation off the old dear's face. Better to let her know there'd been a sighting and she could take what hope she would from that.

Madame B wasn't as easily put off though.

"*Ou?*" she said, looking around my apartment as if it was totally logical to believe I'd found the cat and brought it here.

I forced myself not to point toward the balcony and instead decided this was a good time to pretend not to understand French—my greatest skill so far in this country.

Thankfully, there was a knock at the door and before I could jump up to answer it Merci strode into the living room with a struggling dirty white cat in her arms.

Both old ladies squealed and clapped their hands as Merci deposited the cat into Madame B's lap.

Merci turned to me. "I am sorry. Your door was open and I heard *les soeurs*. You are not minding?"

I grinned at how the old ladies cuddled the cat, relief and delight stamped across their faces.

"No, are you kidding?" I said as I got up to fetch another wine glass. "You're the hero of the hour. Can you stay?"

"If there is wine?" Merci said with a laugh. "But of course!"

As soon as she sat down a blur of black fur shot through the still open door.

"Oh, there's *Neige!*" Merci said. "Now we are a party!"

I glanced at the black cat nosing about my kitchen, clearly looking for his dinner.

"He's called *Neige*?" I asked. "What's that mean in English?"

"Oh, it is the word for snow," Merci said with a laugh as I poured her wine. "The Poupards are being funny, yes?"

I narrowed my eyes at the black cat named Snow and then put a chunk of cheese on a saucer and set it on the floor. Instantly both cats pounced on it.

"So *Neige* is the Poupards' cat?" I asked as the two cats companionably nibbled on the cheese.

"Of course," Merci said. She shook her head and spoke to the sisters and all three of them directed their attention to the voices coming up from the back garden.

"What's happening down there?" I asked. "Do they know yet who it is?"

"I spoke with Eloise," Merci said in a low voice. "She is the sergeant on the case. It is truly terrible." She turned to the elderly sisters and spoke to them. Both of them gasped and Madame C clapped a hand to her heart, her lips trembling.

"The woman they found is Lilou Basso," Merci said.

So I was right. It was a woman.

"Do they have any idea how she got there?" I asked.

"*Non*. But she did not get there by herself!" Merci said with a raised eyebrow.

"So they think it's murder?"

"*Oui*, of course."

"Did you know her?"

"Everyone knew Lilou. She was...not fast in the head, you see."

"Oh."

Somehow that made it worse.

I could see that the Madame Sisters had decided to focus on the return of their cat and not the voices coming from outside or whatever Merci and I were saying. That was probably just as well.

"Did Eloise say how she died?" I asked.

"They don't know yet. They can't get the medical examiner here because of the blackout."

"Yeah, what's the deal with that? Does this happen a lot?"

"Not really. Once in a while we might lose power but the cellphone towers must be down too. Have you tried your phone?"

I nodded and glanced at my phone on the kitchen counter as I felt a tingle of fear.

It's one thing to be in a foreign country with no lights. But not to have access to the world at the push of a button? I realized my palms were damp and I wiped them on my shorts.

"Yeah," I said. "My laptop is dead too."

Merci nodded. "So it is all very strange." She looked around the living room. "You are well prepared for the blackout, I see."

"Where I come from, losing power is practically a weekly occurrence. Atlanta has so many trees that it only takes a spring breeze to bring down major power lines. So I ran to the hardware store and stocked up as soon as I saw the signs."

"Very smart. It is good for *les soeurs* that you did so."

I thought about that for a moment as I watched the old ladies pet the errant Camille. I made a mental note to give them a flashlight and the lantern when it came time to call it a night.

Watching them relax, drink the wine and smile at their beloved kitty, I couldn't help but think that we were all working in the dark with a killer on the loose.

These two old sweeties were lucky to be able to make it up and down the stairs without also having to worry about that too.

It was then that I felt a flinch of sorrow that I wouldn't be around to help them through this until the lights came back on.

❄❄❄❄❄

Luc was walking the perimeter of the garden for the fifth time. Looking up, he saw there were five balconies around the garden. Three were shut tight and his men had confirmed that the apartments were vacant.

Of the other two, one belonged to the American who was here on vacation and the other was owned by a Hugo Remet. Luc had assigned Eloise the job of getting a statement from Monsieur Remet.

As the light diminished in the sky, the flickering glow from the battery-operated lanterns that his team had set up became brighter. Luc walked again toward the body, careful not to come too close so as not to compromise any of the possible evidence.

Because the American had found the body, her footprints would have to be noted and discounted. He didn't seriously consider her a suspect. There was no motive, means or opportunity for her to have killed Lilou.

While Luc didn't have time of death yet, it seemed unlikely that the American could have arrived in Chabanel and murdered someone before unpacking.

Plus, the markings on Lilou's throat pointed to strangulation. That was evident even from six feet away. There was no way a woman as slim as the American—probably no way any woman at all—could have been responsible for that.

"Chief?"

Luc turned to see Eloise standing beside him. Even in the half gloom of the evening and the lanterns, he could see the excitement in her eyes. This would be her first homicide since graduating from the academy.

He wondered if he'd looked that vulture-like when he was her age.

She held out the satellite phone to him. Luc had sent one of the other men back to the station on foot to retrieve it—and any information there about what was happening in Haute Provence that might explain the mysterious blackout.

The fact that Eloise was handing him a satellite phone told him there had been no report back at the station. He took the phone and punched in the code for his superior in Aix, waving Eloise away at the same time.

He waited, his eyes on the balcony above him that he knew belonged to the American woman. There were lights inside and he heard laughter.

"This is Chief Inspector Tourner," a voice barked on the other end.

Luc turned away from the dark facade of the apartment building.

"Jean-Paul," Luc said. "It's Luc DeBray in Chabanel. What is happening?"

A Gallic curse erupted on the line before his supervisor spoke again.

"It's a shit storm, Luc. Reports are coming in but slowly. All comms are down. In fact everything is down."

"What was it?" Luc said, feeling a tightening in his chest. "Was it an EMP?" All the signs pointed to it and he could only hope he was wrong.

"We don't know for sure," Jean-Paul said. "But the word we're hearing is that the lights are out everywhere."

"Where is everywhere?"

Did he mean the whole of the south of France? Surely not.

"All of Europe," Tourner said abruptly. "The UK too."

Susan Kiernan-Lewis

7

No Time Like the Present

Luc stared at the dark computer screen on his desk. He might as well remove it. Even if they got the power grid back up this machine was done.

Even if? He shook his head at his pessimism.

If what Tourner told him last night was true—combined with Luc's own observations—Chabanel and indeed all of France had just entered the New Dark Ages.

It was a miracle it hadn't happened sooner.

Late last night it was finally confirmed that an EMP was the culprit for the new state of crisis that Provence—and indeed all of Europe—currently found itself.

While all the details were still creeping in, the picture that was forming seemed to be that a nuclear bomb had detonated over the Mediterranean yesterday afternoon, creating an electro magnetic pulse that zapped all electronics and vehicles built after 1985—essentially sending them all back to the 1950s.

That is if the 1950s didn't have electricity.

As Luc looked out the picture window this morning onto the Place de le Maire, he couldn't help but feel that the identity of the group or country responsible for the bomb was oddly irrelevant.

Would there be looting in Aix when people realized the current state of things wasn't temporary? Would there be panic and rioting?

He'd already received word last night via the satellite phone—whose charge was nearing its end—that it appeared the US had already descended into chaos and lawlessness.

Or perhaps that was just wishful thinking on the part of Paris?

Luc moved to the picture window and rubbed a tired hand across his face. He didn't normally begin his day without an espresso and something in his stomach.

But things weren't normal.

Since they hadn't been able to remove Lilou Basso's body last night, Luc had been forced to post a guard—old Romeo Remey, who only worked for the gendarmerie part time these days. Today Luc would do what he could to process the crime scene without the benefit of technology —without cameras, footprint casting, or DNA kits.

It was a new world order. A button reset that had wiped out all the technological advances of the last fifty years. One thing was certain, however: there weren't enough police in Aix to handle what would come next. Not once people realized what was happening.

Would Chabanel be any different?

He'd spent the night at the police station and while it had been a quiet night due to no working phones, no fewer than twenty people had knocked on the station door with questions about the blackout. Once news got out about the EMP, he could only imagine how people would react.

Thankfully the Aix-en-Provence Hospital which also served Chabanel had a generator that was still running.

He thought of Lilou Basso. They may never know what happened to her. With so many other pressing problems needing to be solved—problems that dramatically impacted the living—it would be hard to prioritize justice for the dead.

A homicide to be solved without the help of DNA, databases or any sort of forensic science? Nothing but laborious manpower to canvas eyewitnesses and attempt to collect circumstantial evidence. How would his team have time for that?

What will we become now? he couldn't help wondering. In a world coming apart at the seams, what would tiny Chabanel do?

Then he stiffened his spine. It didn't matter *what* they were doing in America or Berlin or Barcelona. Aix would not become lawless and wild, nor would Chabanel.

We are French! We will carry on.

"Chief?"

He turned to see Eloise standing in the door of his office. She looked tired. He resolved to send her home early today so she could get some rest. He would need to lean hard on her and his second-in-command Adrien Matteo in the coming days.

She dropped an envelope on his desk.

"From the mayor," she said. "Do you want me to get coffee?"

Luc smiled tiredly. He knew what the offer must have cost her, but he shook his head.

"What's it like out there this morning?" he said. He had every intention of walking the streets to see for himself. Amazingly, if what he could view from his window was any indication at all, there was very little to distinguish this morning from any other beautiful summer day in Chabanel.

But it was early days yet. Once people learned the truth about what had happened...

"It's quiet," Eloise said. "The cafés are still open. And I saw them setting up the market in the square."

"Good, good."

"What does it mean, Chief?" Eloise's face was pale behind her glasses.

Luc forced a business-like smile for her. "We will weather it," he said simply. No molly-coddling, he thought. No good could come from that.

"I need you to move the body to the Aix hospital morgue," he said.

When Eloise stared at him in confusion, he picked up the envelope from his desk.

"Go to Armand at the Bar á GoGo," he said. "His brother has a horse and wagon. Make arrangements for him to meet you on rue Gaston de Saporta."

"I'm to take the body to the hospital by way of the D7N?" she asked.

Luc glanced at the letter inside the envelope.

"*Oui*," he said. "There will be no traffic."

She turned to go and then stopped.

"One of the witnesses from the case is here to see you. The American."

His eyebrows shot up.

"Yes?"

"She's upset."

Luc looked around his office. A blanket still lay on his couch where he'd slept. An overflowing ashtray was on the side table.

"Show her in."

Luc barely had time to scan his desktop for any sensitive material before Eloise ushered in Jules Hooker dragging her roll-on luggage behind her.

"Madame Hooker?" he said pleasantly, gesturing to a chair.

"Please call me Jules," she said, not sitting. Her knuckles were white where she clutched the handle of her suitcase.

"What is the problem, please?" he asked.

"I think I'm trapped here! I don't understand what's happening but I'm supposed to be at the Marseilles airport in one hour for a flight to the US. Only my phone doesn't work and I can't call a taxi to get to the Aix bus station and there's no American consulate in town."

Luc was surprised he hadn't noticed how vulnerable she looked or how luminous her complexion was. His conversation with her yesterday after she discovered the body had been cut short, true, but perhaps hers was the kind of beauty that moved up on you in stages.

He was well aware that some women were beautiful like a train mowing you down in their path and some presented a slower buildup. Personally, he felt the latter to be much more enduring.

She sat down hard on one of the chairs facing his desk and he had the distinct impression her legs had given out on her.

"I would be wanting to speak to you again in any event, Madame...Jules," he said kindly. "You are an important part of my investigation into a suspicious death."

"Am I a suspect?" she asked, her bottom lip quivering slightly.

"*Non*. But you might have seen something that would be of help."

"I can't be of help. I didn't see anything but an arm and a cat. And I really need to get on that airplane. Can't you help me?"

Luc wondered if she'd noticed that there were no lights on at the police station. True they had battery-operated lanterns in each room but she must know that something unusual had happened.

"I am afraid there will be no flights in or out of France at present."

"What do you mean?" Her voice rose and her eyes darted around the room in mounting agitation. "When can I go home?"

"Madame...Jules, we have experienced an incident here, yes? You are understanding? You cannot leave. You should go back to your apartment—"

"It's not my apartment! I'm only swapping mine with the Poupards."

"Yes, I know this. Go back and wait."

"Wait for what?"

She looked so distraught that it was all Luc could do not to give in to the temptation to assure her that she would be heading home soon. But he could not do that. At best it would be months. At worst, perhaps never. He tapped the envelope on his desk and forced a smile.

"The mayor of Chabanel will speak this evening at the square *de Maire*, yes? Right outside? You will come? It will all be explained then."

Luc stood up to encourage Jules to do the same. She blinked at him as if she didn't understand and then she stood and took the handle of her roll-on luggage.

"Okay," she said in a stunned voice. "Thank you."

She turned and walked slowly out of his office as if hoping he might call her back at any moment to say it had all been a joke.

How he wished he could do exactly that.

※※※※※※

I can't really say how that first day after the EMP passed for me.

I know after paying a visit to the police, I made it back to my apartment and as far as the bedroom before collapsing on the bed in tears. I didn't bother unpacking my suitcase or even locking the front door behind me.

I think I must have been in some sort of a trance—so much so that I fell asleep almost instantly and slept for the rest of the day. When I awoke I prayed that it was all a terrible dream but as I lay in a stranger's bed in my traveling clothes—my shoes still on my feet—and watched the afternoon sun paint the metal bars of the balcony golden red hues I realized that something world-shattering had happened and here I was without even five minutes of access to Fox News or CNN or any other news channel to tell me what the hell it was.

I looked at my watch. Five o'clock. I wasn't sure when the mayor was going to speak but I was pretty sure I wanted to be there when he did. Granted, he or she was certainly going to be speaking in French but it didn't matter. I needed to be around people who were all grappling with the same desperate need for information that I was.

As I lay on the bed, willing myself to get up and find something in the fridge to tide me over, Neige jumped on the bed and settled down by my hip. It was the first friendly gesture he'd made in my direction and it actually brought tears to my eyes.

I reached out to pet him and the motion sent him flying into the other room. I rubbed a budding ache between my eyes with my thumbs.

I'm a reporter. I need information. I need to know what's going on. I need to know that even when there's nothing going on. But I especially need to know *now*.

I straightened the worst of the wrinkles out of my tunic and yoga pants and went to the kitchen where I drank the rest of the orange juice in the fridge straight from the carton. The sugar in the drink gave me a mental boost and I felt a lot better. I was still making a conscious effort not to look out my balcony but I wasn't hearing any voices any more so I assumed the police had finally removed the body.

The body.

I took in a steadying breath.

I can't believe any of this is happening—whatever this is. First a dead body and now some kind of countrywide brownout.

I saw my suitcase and my carryon where I'd left them in the living room. I pulled my cellphone out of the carryon and looked at it. There was no sense in carrying it because I had no way of charging it up. I took a few euros out of my wallet and jammed them into the pocket of my stretchy hoodie jacket. I'd dressed for comfort not style that morning since I thought I'd be lounging in an Airbus recliner all day.

A knock at my door had me turning that way when it opened. Merci stood there.

"*Bonsoir*, Jules!" she said. "Are you going to the village meeting tonight?"

It was a relief to see her. Not just because she spoke English but...well, no, mainly that was the reason.

"I am going," I said, meeting her at the door. "And I could really use someone to translate for me. Have you checked on the Madame twins?"

Merci laughed. "You Americans and your nicknames. Yes, they are fine for now. They will be glad to see that you have not left."

"Yeah, well, I guess, we're all in this together," I said as I stepped out into the hall and pulled my apartment door shut behind me. "Whatever *this* is."

8

The Low Down

The village meeting looked more like a summer festival but I guess that's because it was France. It was held in front of city hall, the big building with the clock on it in front of the war memorial.

There was a whole bunch of open containers in the crowd and a whole lot of opinions being shouted out about a wide variety of subjects.

Alcohol and politics. Always a great combination, don't you think?

The one thing that didn't jive with the whole summer festival vibe was the creeping panic that seemed to be pinging off everybody in the crowd. At least two hundred people were crammed into the town square.

A small wooden stage had been erected in front of the mayor's office. I'd only been in France two days in my entire life but already I knew that the French were masters at creating a tableau, knocking it down and creating something totally different. An hour ago this square had been an outdoor restaurant complete with checkered tablecloths.

Now it was a spotlessly swept town square with more people in it than your average Wal-Mart.

Whatever comfort I'd felt by hanging with Merci dissolved the minute I saw the somewhat agitated crowd and also because she ditched me as soon as we got to the square.

I moved through the crowd as close to the front of the stage as I could. There were a few chairs on the stage and a battery-operated megaphone next to a podium. I spotted Luc DeBray immediately.

Even though he was on the stage he looked completely unselfconscious. He had his weight on one hip—and one hand too—but instead of looking fey or effeminate he looked incredibly full of himself and I mean that in a totally good way.

The babble of French spoken around me reminded me of how comforting I'd recently discovered it was to hear language spoken that I didn't have to assign meaning to but it also reminded me that I was not going to be able to understand anything that was being said here tonight. I'd counted on Merci to translate for me.

Luc was talking to a middle-aged woman who looked very grim but also like she was in charge. It hadn't occurred to me that the Mayor of Chabanel might be a woman and for some reason I felt better knowing that.

I looked around to see if anyone was covering this. Even without a way to print a newspaper surely there would be a re-telling of what happened here today? But I couldn't see anyone who looked like a reporter.

I only saw fear and confusion. And drinking.

Again, not a great situation for a crowd mentality.

I glanced at my watch and as I waited for the meeting to begin I noticed there were people in the crowd handing out fliers. Having no real hope of being able to understand the flyers any more that I expected to understand the speech, I still held out my hand for one and was delighted to see that it seemed to be a transcript of tonight's speech. In French on one side and English on the other.

"Bonsoir! Merci d'être venu ce soir."

I looked up to see that the older woman was standing at the podium with the megaphone to her mouth. Luc and two other men stood behind her.

I ran my finger down the English transcription and hoped I could tell by certain English-French words or the crowd's reaction where the mayor was in her speech.

I shouldn't have been surprised that the Mayor—Madame Lola Beaufait—was beautiful. She was impeccably dressed in a dove gray Chanel suit with matching pumps.

Perfect for stepping up in a post-apocalyptic world.

While it was true her face showed her age even from where I stood, I could sense the kindness and wisdom in her eyes. If this was a politician, she was like none I'd ever seen before.

The crowd might not have been as impressed as I was because they began to talk—loudly. I wasn't sure whether this was how political discourse was handled in France or whether today was different.

Let's face it. Today was different.

"I hope to be able to answer most of your questions," the mayor said as I read along. "But before I do, I have a statement that may answer many of them.

"I have spoken to Aix today via a military field phone about our situation here in Chabanel, in fact in all of Provence, and I will tell you what I know and what I can promise you is being done about it. First, let me say we are luckier than many villages in France."

The crowd definitely reacted to that because up to now we didn't know it wasn't just us here in Chabanel. I felt myself jostled by the mob.

Would they storm the stage? Was it their intention to beat a different answer out of their elected official?

I glanced at Luc and saw that he was scanning the crowd intently but didn't appear to be worried. I took that as a good sign.

"I have been informed," Madame Beaufait continued, "that at sixteen hundred hours yesterday, a nuclear detonation over the Mediterranean near Cannes created an electro magnetic pulse which interacted with the earth's magnetic field."

The crowd collectively gasped and began to murmur loudly.

"While this caused no harm to people or animals," the mayor said quickly, "the resulting massive overload of our electrical circuits stripped us of most of our electronics, as well as most of our working vehicles."

An elderly gentleman in front of me yelled out to the stage and as I watched the people around him nodding their heads at whatever it was he'd said, I felt a hand on my elbow.

I turned, expecting to see Merci—as she was the only person in Chabanel whom I knew might possibly touch me —and was surprised to see instead a tall man who was looking at the speaking Frenchman as he spoke to me in English.

"The old guy wants to know why his 1965 Saab still runs when his neighbor's brand new Renault doesn't?" He glanced down at me and smiled. "Hello. I'm Jim Anderson."

"You're American!"

"Hell of a thing, isn't it? I live on the outskirts of Chabanel. I'll be happy to translate the crowd noise for you."

Before I could reply, a shrill woman's voice shouted over the crowd.

"She wants to know when the lights will go back on," Jim said.

When the mayor addressed the speaker, Jim turned to me and smiled apologetically. "The mayor says no time soon."

That got the crowd going and if I were honest, Jim's words put a chill down my spine too. He'd removed his hand from my arm but I was glad of the physical presence of him next to me.

"Now the mayor is asking everyone to please remain calm. She says at the very least it will take three years to rebuild the destroyed transformers—and then only if there's a country able to manufacture them who was not also hit."

He frowned. "Ouch. I could have gone all day without hearing that. She says Paris is still attempting to ascertain how widespread the damage is."

"I'm Jules Hooker," I said. "How did you know I was American?"

"I'm one of the admins for the local ex-pat group here in Provence. Luc DeBray ran by my place this afternoon to ask me to keep an eye out for you."

"You know DeBray?"

"Of course. He's a good guy. Going to have his hands full now though. Oh, the mayor's talking again."

I glanced down at my handout and saw that she was back to the script—at least until somebody else asked a question.

"Here in Chabanel as well as all of Aix-en-Provence," she said, "we have suffered a loss of infrastructure and I can warn you that much will be different going forward as a result of that. And before you ask nobody knows for how long. As the mayor of Chabanel, I am urging all shop and café owners to remain open as usual. Different methods for refreshing your inventory are being explored at the moment.

"But I can promise you that if you sell wine, you will have wine on your shelves. If you sell bread, you will have access to flour and yeast and sugar. If you serve meals, you will be able to replenish your supplies to continue serving meals. It will be business as usual in Chabanel."

A man shouted out something and the crowd and Jim laughed.

"That guy wants to know if they'll be paid for those services in smiles."

The mayor responded and Jim said, "Beaufait said he'll be paid in a variety of ways."

"Uh-oh," I said. "That's a little vague."

The crowd must have thought so too because several people began booing. Jim shook his head.

"They all want to know if their money is still good and while Beaufait says yes, they think she hesitated before she said it."

"Do you trust her?"

Jim shrugged. He wasn't bad looking at all. Tall, which I like. And green eyes. A bonus.

"I guess so," he said. "I mean, she's still a politician, right? Oh, now she's saying that there will be an *additional* kind of currency. Yeah, she doesn't want to go too far down that road."

More people shouted more questions.

"People want to know if their money is safe in the banks," Jim said. "She's telling them the banks will reopen tomorrow."

I heard someone yell out something that sounded like *ATM* and Beaufait shook her head.

"She's telling them that they'll have to come into the bank like in the old days. No more ATM machines."

As the shouts from the crowd got louder, Jim squinted at the handout.

"It looks like a lot of their questions would be answered if they'd just let her speak. But that's the French for you."

I glanced at the handout and read a version of what it sounded like people were asking her.

Q: What about the petrol stations? I can't get petrol!

M: Because the pumps depend on electricity, I am sorry, for now we will not be able to access petrol.

Q: And the grocery stores? Already the meat and milk are rotting!

M: At the moment we have no refrigeration. Food shops like Casino are first on our list for receiving help with preserving food.

Q: What about refrigeration in our homes?

M: You will have to find other methods. My office will release a list of various alternatives. For example root cellars. It is true that your milk will not be as cold as you would like but this is where we are now.

Q: I need to visit my mother in Lyons! When will the trains be running again?

M: They won't. The rail lines were conductors for the EMP. Our trains are permanently stopped.

I felt suddenly overwhelmed—by the crowd and by what I was hearing. When DeBray told me this morning what had happened I thought I'd more or less processed the horror of it but I wasn't even close. As I stood there with a whole crowd of people totally different from me—Jim as the only exception—I never felt so alone in my life.

"Here's the part where she talks about who did this to us," Jim said. "Try not to look too American for the next few minutes."

"Why?" I said, startled. "Do people think *we* did this?"

"At this point," the mayor said, "we do not know who is responsible for the EMP or even if there will be follow-up attacks. Our government has announced that it considers the attack an act of war and once we ascertain who launched it, we will respond accordingly."

"On bicycles?" someone yelled. Even I understood that.

"*Non*, Philippe," another man yelled to him. "I'm sure the military has access to scooters!"

"Let us focus on our own little part of the world, eh?" Beaufait said sternly. "The food markets and shops will be given first priority for help with distribution and shipping. Money will inevitably become less important. I would ask you to be looking for ways to barter or exchange services for the things you need. If you have a skill—or are able to help in ways that were perhaps not valued before—you will be in an improved position than before."

"In our new world the blacksmith will outrank the banker," Jim said in a low voice.

"*Comment?*" several people yelled out.

I looked at the handout and saw the mayor was back to her talking points.

"Finding sources of water, purifying that water, taking care of the horses which will now be needed to draw the wagons for transportation of goods and people. Those who are handy with fashioning items from existing materials—taking scraps of junk, perhaps to create a tool—will rise in value accordingly. As will those who know the old ways of doing things. These people will become our most important assets now.

"A list of needed skills and services will be posted outside my office. All those who feel they may contribute in these ways are urged to apply. You will be paid in special privileges and daily meals. As for our medical needs in Chabanel, the hospital in Aix has a working generator. Drug shipments and other necessary items for the hospital will take priority along with potable water and food for the community. With the exception of a few government buildings, the hospital will be the only structure in the Aix commune—of which of course we in Chabanel belong—that has electricity—at least for now—and so entrance there will be carefully monitored."

"She means not everyone will be allowed in," Jim said.

"My office will disseminate posters throughout the streets of Chabanel to notify you of any important news. You may contact my office by writing me a letter..."

"*Est-ce que cela est vraiment possible?*" the crowd exploded in astonishment.

"...as I am assured that the postal service will continue uninterrupted if more slowly. For now there will be no need for postage. You may of course hand deliver your requests or questions directly to my office.

"*Et les gendarmes?*" a woman's voice called out.

"The police will function as before," Beaufait said, gesturing to Luc behind her. "They will have mobile radios to keep in touch with each other and their base of command. Their power will understandably enlarge in order to accommodate new issues as they arrive. I hope I don't have to say that looting or theft will be dealt with in extreme measures. The laws for Chabanel are being changed as we speak to reflect our new situation."

I looked at Luc's face but his expression gave nothing away. A good poker face is probably essential in his job.

"Police Chief Luc DeBray is in charge and tasked with keeping the peace and trust me when I say that he will do exactly that. I tell you, good people of Chabanel, that we will not descend into chaos like some other countries are doing! Those countries that allowed their citizenry to arm will turn into warring factions, neighbors killing neighbors. We will not allow that to happen in France. We will go on as before. The rules are still the rules. Break them and you will be punished."

The crowd was quiet, listening as if stunned. I knew exactly how they felt.

"Very soon my office will hand out a ration of kerosene or other burning oil for each family in Chabanel. Use this fuel sparingly as I do not anticipate being able to offer more any time soon. As we go forward, I will keep you updated on what other measures we will do to keep Chabanel as it has always been—except without smart phones and television sets.

"For those with special considerations—newborns, the elderly, the ill or handicapped—please see my office. For everyone else, be prudent, be safe, and have faith in your country. We will survive this. We will triumph over this. On that, I have no doubt. Viva la France! I will take any remaining questions now."

As the crowd surged forward toward the stage, shouting out questions, Jim pulled me away from the crush.

"I have a question," he said as he leaned over to talk in my ear over the clamor of the surrounding crowd. "Are you interested in getting a drink somewhere? I hear all the bars are going to be open."

9

All Together Now

I have to admit that any other time while the world was ending a drink would have sounded like a great idea but now that I knew what was more or less going on I wanted to check in with the old biddies Madames Cazaly and Becque to make sure they were okay.

Jim was cool about it and I did my best to make it clear that I'd totally be up for it another time.

But I think the key phrase among all that is the one that goes: *now that I knew what was going on.* Because now that I did, I was so freaked out I could barely find my way back to the apartment without losing my mind to terror and wild imaginings and so I could only guess how the two sisters must be feeling.

My thoughts were a whirl by the time I turned down my street—totally dark as I knew it would be. Jim seemed to think the US was the reason for the bomb going off over Europe and I had to admit that sounded plausible. If I—as a red-blooded, flag-waving Yankee Doodle type—thought so, you could bet everyone here in France did too.

I shivered at the thought of my neighbors having an outlet in the form of myself for their frustration at being in the dark, their ATMs shut down, their beers warm and their cars kaput.

Who could blame them for wanting to take a shot at me?

But I also worried about Atlanta. What about Gilbert? Or CeCe? Were Atlantans ripping up Peachtree Street or sitting back sipping Coca-Cola as if nothing had happened?

Had anything happened back there?

I pushed open the heavy apartment building door and felt my heart fluttering in my throat. The whole world was dark now and locks didn't mean much any more.

"*Merci, est-ce toi, chérie?*" an elderly female voice called out tremulously.

"No, it's just me," I called back and was rewarded with the sounds of both old dears squealing with delight. In a second one of them had the beam of the flashlight I'd given them last night pointed at me as I came up the stairs.

They met me at the door to my apartment, which was open. I have no idea how they got into my place since I was sure I'd locked it before I left. Probably the Poupards, who I was seriously beginning to hate when I wasn't worrying about them being all alone in Atlanta, had given them a key.

The first thing I did was make sure the battery-powered lantern was positioned on the kitchen counter to illuminate the entire apartment. Then I set about making dinner to keep my mind occupied so I wouldn't go screaming out the door in the throes of a panic attack.

An all too likely possibility.

It would've really helped about now if one of the old girls could speak my language. They nattered on quite a bit but didn't seem at all concerned about not getting a coherent response from me.

There was no sense looking in the fridge or finding anything that required cooking. I saw there was a fresh baguette on the counter so one of the sisters must have gone out today.

I pulled out the rest of the cheese from last night plus what was left of the salami. When I remembered buying this stuff the day before yesterday and how I was so sure it would all rot in my fridge before it gotten eaten, my hands began to shake.

The electricity was not coming back on. The stove was never going to work. My phone was not going to power up again. My laptop was a permanent boat anchor.

I took in a long breath, closed my eyes, and breathed out slowly. When I did I felt a firm hand on my back. When I opened my eyes I saw that Madame Becque was beside me, her eyes probing.

"*Ça va?*" she said.

"Yep. Absolutely."

How do I tell them that this is the new normal?

Madame Becque's eyes were warm and for a moment I got a flash of memory of my mother. I'd spoken to her a couple of months ago but hadn't seen her in years. We'd never been close. My dad died when I was twenty-two. A year later my mom married our insurance agent and moved to Toronto.

Sound and activity at the front door pulled me out of my thoughts and I looked up to see Merci and a man I'd seen her talking with at the town meeting. She had her arm looped through his.

He was handsome and big with a loose grin but something about the way he was with Merci told me they were not together.

"Jules!" Merci called, pulling the man into the kitchen with her. "I lost you in the square! So many people!"

"No worries," I said, piling the various wedges and chunks of Roquefort and *chèvre* onto a tray and handing it to Madame Becque. "It was pretty wild."

"Jules, this is my brother Guy."

Guy reached a massive hand out and we shook.

"*Enchantez*," he said, his eyes smiling at me.

"Me, too," I said idiotically. I don't know what there is about a good looking guy who gives me any attention—even in the middle of a world-order meltdown—that tends to derail me.

We moved into the living room where Madame Becque and Madame Cazaly were setting out the cheese and salami. Guy had a bottle of wine with him that I hadn't noticed before and Merci grabbed the bread from the kitchen counter.

I can't even begin to say how much it helped for all of us to sit there with one lantern, two flashlights and a half dozen candles, the balcony door open and the night breeze wafting in. Merci was the only one who spoke English but she translated and so it felt very much like I was getting to know the people in my living room.

My living room.

Oh my God. I can't live in France!

Just when the reality of my situation would slam into me, something would happen—Neige scratched Guy or Merci dropped a wine glass or one of the old ladies would clap their hands about something—and I'd ease out of it.

Good thing too. Or I'd probably be jumping off the aforementioned balcony.

I hadn't eaten all day and I was hungry. But I was also aware that this food might have to last awhile. As soon as that thought came to me, I lost my appetite.

Hey, maybe the apocalypse will be a great way to get rid of that last five pounds I've been working on.

"Jules?" Merci said, pointing to my now empty wineglass.

I nodded as she refilled it.

"How did you learn to speak English so well?" I asked.

"Well, they teach it in school although you wouldn't know that by talking to my brother."

Guy shrugged. "I understood you," he said in English, his pronunciation absolutely adorable. "A little." He made it sound like "lee-tle."

"But mostly I learned it from my boyfriend," Merci said. "He was a student at the Aix University. We were together for nearly two years."

"What happened to him?"

Merci shrugged. "He graduated."

I decided this wasn't the time to ask for details.

Madame Cazaly tapped me on the knee and said something to me so I automatically turned to Merci.

"She wants to know if your family back in the US is okay."

I looked back at Madame C. Her brow was wrinkled in concern.

At least she doesn't blame me for all this.

Yet.

"I don't know," I said. "My dad died years ago and my mom and I don't talk much. I can only hope she's okay."

As Merci translated my words, Madame C nodded sadly. When she did it occurred to me that she would be old enough to have lived through World War II. She would remember the Nazi occupation.

It made me want to make sure that both she and Madame B didn't have to hear more than they really needed to about our situation. It made me want to make sure that they were going to be okay.

"They took the body away today," Merci said solemnly, nodding at the balcony.

"I thought so. I slept most of the day but it was really quiet out there. How did they do it?"

"You won't believe it. Horse and wagon! But I talked with Eloise and she said the police would be getting vehicles soon."

"Well, that's comforting, I guess. As long as it's not a Smart Car or something."

Merci giggled and covered her mouth.

"Can you imagine Chief DeBray in a Smart Car?" she said, giggling all over again.

"Yeah, he's got long legs," I said. "It'd be interesting watching him get in and out. What do you know about him?"

"Aside from how sexy he is? Not much. He came to Chabanel four years ago, I think from Alsace. If he's dating anyone in the village I haven't heard about it."

"*Would* you hear about it?"

Merci grinned. "Of course, dear Jules! If it's gossip, I make it my business to know it! Besides, Eloise goes to my favorite bar sometimes and she will talk."

"But there's nothing to say about DeBray?"

"So far, no. *Quelle dommage!*"

Guy went into the kitchen and began rummaging around in the drawers. I turned back to Merci.

"What's your brother do?"

Merci followed my eyes as I watched him.

"He is a fix-it man, you know? He is who they were talking about. Before the EMP he is making no money, yes? A little bit of this, a little bit of that. But now? Now I think Guy will be the new mayor of Aix!"

"He should register his skillset with the mayor's office in Chabanel," I said.

"He will. My mother will see that he does!" She laughed again.

"Didn't tonight freak you out?" I asked in a low voice, my eyes on the twins in case they were able to understand more than I thought. "I can't believe half of what the mayor said."

"I know."

"The police will have their hands full with all this. There's no way they'll be able to sort out what happened to poor Lilou."

Merci cocked her head to look at me. "You care about her."

Her words made me realize that I really did. I wasn't aware to what extent until that moment.

"I do. I mean, I should any way but because I was the one who found her and because she was...slow, I can't get her out of my mind."

"I think you are right about the police. They do not have their microscopes and computers to solve this murder, eh? They don't know how to do it unless they can call for their labs."

Was that true, I wondered? It made sense. What with all the advancements in criminal and forensic science in the last twenty years it made complete sense that the old-fashioned way of deciphering clues in a homicide investigation had been lost.

Did Luc even know how to do it in today's new world?

I'd bet a thousand euros he didn't.

Guy came back to the living room with a large plastic bottle in his hands and a piece of cloth tied to the top. He presented it to me and spoke in very rapid French so I did my best to nod and smile as if I knew what the hell he was saying and waited for Merci to tell me.

"It's a charcoal filter!" she said, handing it to me. "You pour the water in here and let it sift through and then it's okay to drink!"

I looked at the bottle and knew I should feel elation at having a device that would help me safely drink contaminated water. But all I felt was a searing anguish that I now lived in a situation that required me to think about such things.

"He knows all kinds of stuff like this," Merci said proudly.

"Thank you, Guy," I said. "*Merci beaucoup.*"

A sudden sound outside in the hall made Merci jump up and when she pulled open the door I was surprised to see the very same man who'd stopped me in the street yesterday after I'd found the body and stalked me at the market. I was so startled to see him that I grabbed Guy's arm.

Merci spoke a few words to the man who shrugged and lumbered off. When she came back she made a face and spoke to Guy in what sounded like very disparaging terms.

"Who was that?" I asked.

"That was Hugo," Merci said. "He lives in the building. Not very friendly but harmless."

I wasn't sure I felt comfortable taking her word for that. I found myself wondering where Hugo was the afternoon Lilou went missing.

As Merci settled back on the couch, Guy produced another bottle of wine from his jacket and the sisters clapped their hands as if they were eight year olds at a birthday party. I supposed that, to the French, someone brandishing a surprise bottle of wine is probably a lot like that.

As he refilled my glass, Guy spoke to Mercy but looked at me.

"My brother wants to know if you're interested in getting some news from the States," Merci said.

"Are you serious?" I spoke to Guy and he laughed, accurately picking up the meaning of my words.

"He knows someone," Merci said, as she loaded up a wedge of triple cream Camembert on a piece of bread.

"What do you mean? There's no news now. No TV, no radio. How?"

Guy grinned and put his hand on Merci's knee to stop her from speaking for him.

"This someones has a radio," he said in English.

"A radio? How is that—"

"A ham radio."

Susan Kiernan-Lewis

10

To Market, To Market

The next morning I knew only two things for sure.

Well, *three* if you count my new knowledge that I shouldn't knock off two bottles of wine largely on my own.

One, I had to find a job. And two, the Chabanel police did not have the resources to investigate Lilou Basso's murder.

Do you see where I'm going with this?

The fact is, for whatever reason I woke up with the one thing that everyone always hopes to wake up to no matter if they're living in a posh gated community in Buckhead or a post-apocalyptic world in the South of France.

I woke up with a purpose.

I mean, of course a purpose beyond not starving to death or seeing that the old biddies didn't starve to death.

I was going to find out who killed Lilou Basso.

Just thinking the words put an extra bounce in my step as I gathered up pens and notepads from my luggage and gave my makeup one last glance in the mirror. It was clear that Luc DeBray had no time to devote to an investigation. Not with the whole world crashing down on his shoulders.

Things like murder and robberies would understandably fall to the wayside. And while logical given the limited manpower, it was especially unfortunate because the bad guys were no doubt counting on it.

I mean, what kind of mayhem would *you* commit if you knew you couldn't be caught? If you knew the police were too busy to look for you?

I stiffened my spine as I gathered my things to prepare for the day.

No sir, I may not have a paying job. I may not speak the language or even know where my next meal was coming from. But by God I have a roof over my head, a budding friendship with a lady who can keep me stocked in cheese, and a city where you could still get a perfectly baked butter croissant any time of the day or night. It could be worse and I was determined to be grateful for that.

I also resolved as I stared at my bedraggled reflection in the cracked mirror in the Poupard's tiny bathroom that just because I was now living in a post-apocalyptic scenario was no reason not to continue to keep up appearances.

The fact is I love clothes and back in Atlanta I spent a good chunk of my paycheck each month on them. Don't get me wrong. I'm not a snob or anything. I just have a certifiable addiction for really nice Italian shoes and designer bags.

I don't have a model's body in that I'm not tall but I'm not chunky either. I've got dark wavy hair to my shoulders, decent skin and blue eyes. Clothes look good on me and I'd fallen in love long ago with the delectable difference between ready to wear and off the rack.

If I were to tell you that I had an outfit in mind for my *going out to find truth for Lilou*, you'd think I was crazy. But in my view there was plenty of time to dress á la Mad Max in the coming days if that's how things shook out but in the meanwhile, while the cafés and the shops were still operational, I was dressing the part.

The weather today was classic summer in the south of France—breezy with a hot sun expected—so I wore my channeling-Bardot-espadrilles with a vintage but no-name sundress I'd gotten at an Atlanta flea market two summers ago. The Poupards kept a wicker basket in the kitchen that I carried with me and went out to see for myself that Chabanel was behaving in the manner that our mayor had asked us.

Look at me already feeling like one of the team. Just thinking the words *our mayor* and *us* made me want to cry.

Chabanel had two bakeries or *boulangeries* and as I passed them I saw that they were both open. I was dying for an almond croissant but since I had a grand total of two hundred euros to last me throughout the apocalypse, I decided to refrain.

Passing up the cafés was a little harder. I'm not sure how the coffee was being brewed without electricity but it smelled absolutely wonderful as I passed the first café I came to.

I was also buoyed along by the appreciative looks that I received—once again confirming that dressing nicely matters no matter the occasion or situation.

I reached the outdoor market at rue de Long and rue Frabrot. As I saw the crowd of people—everyone with bulging baskets of food, cheese and sausages I thought Mayor Beaufait would be so proud.

We can do this, I thought. *We can totally do this*.

I went first to the fishmonger's stand because I had this idea that a nice big fish would be something I could eat but that would also feed Neige. As I paid out the precious euros for the fish, it occurred to me that feeding Neige at all might be a little extravagant considering there was every reason to believe we'd all be living like the Walking Dead by the weekend.

Packing the fish away in my basket made me think of my own kitty, Hamish back in Atlanta. Was he okay? Would the Poupards take care of him? Would they *eat* him?

"Jules!"

I looked up to see Katrine, my friend from the cheese stand waving me over. I joined her and was shocked and delighted when she reached over and kissed me on both cheeks.

"You look gorgeous, *chérie*," Katrine said, beaming. "Taking the end of the world in stride I see?"

"Did you hear the mayor speak last night?" I glanced around to see that her booth looked exactly as it had been before the EMP. The goat cheese packets were tucked in stark white paper cones, the goat cheese was stacked in pyramids and the triple creams and the *Tomme de Savoie* which was so buttery and rich and was quickly becoming my favorite were displayed in little wicker baskets.

"I was at home with the little ones," Katrine said, "but my husband Gaultier was there. It is scary, no?"

As she spoke she gathered up a sampling of cheeses and put them in a paper bag, efficiently twisting the ends and handing it to me. I reached for my coin purse but she waved me away.

"Not this time, my friend."

"Thanks, Katrine. Without the use of an ATM, I'm not sure how I'm going to make my euros last." I looked around at the bustling market. "Guess I'm the only one worried about that."

Katrine shrugged. "I am sure it will all sort itself out. For today, my sales have been better than ever! And Mayor Beaufait has promised Gaultier access to a horse and wagon to bring our products in from the farms outside Chabanel. Is good, no?"

"Yeah, no, it is good," I said. "So how are people paying you?"

"With money, so far. A few have offered a lewd act or two, *n'est-ce pas*? Many of my countrymen are so amusing."

"So it hasn't come to bartering yet?"

She gestured to a bag behind her. "I took a hand-knitted shawl for a wheel of *Pont l'Evêque* this morning."

"Do you really think it's possible for us to live without money or electricity?"

She shrugged. "*Pourquoi pas*? My great-grandparents had neither and they were happy and well fed I can tell you!"

After a little more conversation along those lines, I said goodbye to Katrine, and I have to admit I felt better. The market really did look like what I imagined a typical shopping day would look like and so far nobody looked like they were starving to death—or panicking.

Was this just me being too American and overthinking things? Or had the world really come to an end and the French were doing their *eat, drink and eat some more* thing and it was all working out?

As I turned away from the market I couldn't help but wonder what I would have to sell—beyond the obvious—once my euros ran out. Maybe being a foreigner I would qualify as one of the mayor's charity cases. I had to admit that without any language skills, I was pretty useless. As I walked through the market, I thought of the old ladies back at the apartment and how helpless they were now and I felt a shiver of resolve that somehow I'd find the way to earn money to keep us all afloat.

Somehow.

I left rue Fabrot and the market and walked down several side streets. The shops were all closed—many of them had boards across the doors and windows to discourage looting—but surprisingly most restaurants were still open. I hesitated in the doorway of one and was astonished to see that the interior seemed well lit. The aroma of roasting meat drifted out onto the street.

How were they cooking the food?

"You are looking better today," a deep voice in heavily accented English said to me, making me jump and nearly drop my fish basket. I turned to see Luc DeBray at my elbow where he'd just materialized.

"I am sorry to startle you. I thought you saw me."

"No, I was in another world," I said. "Or maybe I was just *wishing* I was in another world. How are they cooking the food without electricity?"

He peered into the restaurant.

"They probably have a grill. If it's gas they'll be fine until they run out of fuel. After that they will have to make other arrangements."

"Like what? Cooking over an open pit?"

He grinned and I realized it was the first time I'd seen him smile. He had nice teeth to go with his full lips. I blushed at the thought.

"*Mais non*, the city will work to keep all cafés and restaurants supplied as much as possible. Our working cafés are the heartbeat of Chabanel. People need a place to gather."

"So the city has enough gas or whatever to supply everyone?"

"Probably not. But there is a black market already set up on the roundabout outside the village. Batteries, oil, petrol and many other things can be obtained there."

"Wow. Is that illegal? You called it a black market."

He shrugged. "We will monitor it to see if it serves a purpose or not."

"It looks like I'm stuck here for awhile," I said, not knowing what else to say. I was tempted to ask him if he wanted to have a cup of coffee but the language barrier wasn't the only impasse to my understanding the French.

"I am sorry," he said and he did look sorry.

"Can I ask you how the investigation is going on Lilou Basso's murder?"

I'd clearly taken him by surprise with that one. His mouth nearly fell open and the atmosphere between us changed from amiable to something a whole lot colder.

"Did you know Mademoiselle Basso?" he asked as if he'd just adjusted the interrogation lamp over a metal table and was getting ready to dust off his thumbscrews.

"You know very well I didn't. That doesn't mean I'm not interested in the case."

"The *case*?"

"Look, it's just that I can see you're pretty busy these days what with the world ending and all."

"We have everything well in hand. I must ask you not to interfere, Madame Hooker."

My cheeks burned as he turned on his heel and marched off. His rebuff embarrassed me because he not only cut off our conversation but also because I'm almost positive he knew the connotation of my last name in English.

If I were a cartoon character there would have been a very serious storm cloud over my head as I watched him stride away.

Although, honestly, it *was* a very nice rear view of a man striding away.

But still! Grrrr!

Just as I was about to walk on, I caught a glimpse of Hugo standing on the corner across the street. He was half turned away from me but there was no doubt that unctuous grease spot was him.

He looked agitated. He glanced over his shoulder and I quickly turned my back to appear to be looking at a postcard carousel by an open *tabac*. When I looked again, he was looking around as if to ensure he wasn't being followed, and then he hurried down a side alley.

So naturally I followed him.

Susan Kiernan-Lewis

11

Trusty Sidekick Wanted

Here's where I was ready to channel my inner Nancy Drew.

I tried to remember if I'd ever read a story where Nancy was attempting to tail a suspect while toting a redolent basket of sea bass.

Cue the ravenous street cats, I thought as I crossed the street.

I don't know why this guy set my teeth on edge. Maybe it was his long greasy hair or his maniacal, shifty eyes. Maybe it was the way he was always licking his lips in that gross *I'm going to eat you* way of his. Maybe it was because he was the first person I'd run into after discovering Lilou's body but whatever it was I could not put away the idea that he was the murderer.

Hey, instincts count for something too, you know.

After his initial pantomime of someone looking around to see if anyone was following him, Hugo became amazingly single-minded and didn't look behind him once. That was a good thing since there were surprisingly few objects for me to hide behind and the alley he had gone down was narrow.

If you didn't count the cursing when I stubbed my toe on a particular prominent edge of cobblestone, it was also pretty quiet. Hugo must be somewhat deaf. Either that or he knew I was behind him and was happily luring me straight to his lair to do God knows what to me.

All I knew for sure was that a guy who looked that nervous and shifty must be a thread that needed pulling.

I was actually envisioning him leading me back to an abandoned garage where I'd find the skeletons of all his other victims along with a few damning souvenirs so that even a non-CSI French Barney Fife like Luc DeBray would have no problem connecting the dots.

As I followed Hugo I was already congratulating myself on cracking the case when Hugo stopped suddenly. Thankfully, there was a tiny shop I could dart into and I did just that before he could turn around. I waited a few seconds and then peered out the shop window over the trays of tarts and colorful macarons on display. *Big surprise. I've discovered yet another bakery.*

"*Puis-je vous aider, Madame?*" the proprietor sang out to me.

"Uh, just looking, *merci beaucoup*," I said. I could barely see Hugo. He was standing in the alley, looking up at the windows.

I could hear the woman baker moving toward me from around the counter—probably to make sure I wasn't about to run off with a baguette from the window display. The last thing I wanted to do was spend one of my precious euros for bread I didn't really want. But neither did I want to reveal myself to Hugo by stepping back out into the alley.

"Madame?"

I glanced at the baker, a stout, stern-faced woman with a rolling pin in her hands.

Wow. Way to intimidate the paying customers, I thought. I hurriedly pointed to a random baguette in the window and reached for my coin purse—all of which seemed to put her in a better mood.

As soon as I paid for the baguette, I stepped back into the alley to confirm what I'd already guessed: Hugo had disappeared.

Annoyed, I settled the fish basket at my feet and sat at one of the two extremely tiny bistro tables in front of the bakery. I ripped off a piece of the still warm bread and it was several long moments before the ecstasy of the taste experience allowed me to gather my thoughts enough to think about what my morning had thus far revealed.

First, I think I have a friend in Katrine. For whatever reason, she'd taken a shine to me and you could do worse than have a cheesemonger like you during an apocalypse.

Second, Luc DeBray also seemed to like me although he had gone instantly sour when I mentioned Lilou Basso's murder investigation. Either that meant he was insecure about the case or he was the murderer. Yeah, probably the first thing.

Third, Hugo my neighbor had opportunity and means to kill poor Lilou. As for motive, you only had to look at him to see he was a sleaze and a perv. I know the police aren't supposed to profile but being a civilian I did feel like I might be allowed to.

Besides, everybody knows if a thing smells like a fish and swims like a fish, it was probably, you know, something that belonged in an aquarium.

A few people walked by me but no one went into the bakery. I wondered what kind of business this place normally did and if they'd possibly be able to survive our new post-EMP world.

Thinking of our new world order reminded me that I had a date. I glanced at my watch and picked up my fish basket.

A date with a very cute guy and a ham radio.

Susan Kiernan-Lewis

12

The Truth Hurts

Luc sat at his desk in the Chabanel *police municipale*. There was a lot more room on the desk now that the computer terminal was gone. In its place he had a growing stack of paper file folders.

Before this week the police station only had himself and two other officers, Eloise Basile and Adrien Matteo, plus one part-time man and a part-time secretary. He'd had to ask the secretary, old Madame Gabin to work full time at least for awhile.

These file folders weren't going to compile themselves.

The amount of work—now that the lights were out and the machines were silent—was staggering. Just getting and receiving communications from Aix was a complex and time-consuming ordeal.

Luc had been promised working vehicles but so far nothing had shown up. He'd had to requisition the use of old Monsieur Flic's 1965 Aston Martin DB5 in order to do basic patrols around the village perimeter. And in the meantime it seemed as if no fewer than half the village had come knocking on his door.

As it was, both Eloise and Matteo were out attempting to calm the population as they responded to the various complaints that were rolling in.

Luc's eyes fell on the file with the fresh new label that read, *Lilou Marguerite Basso*.

And on top of everything they had a homicide to solve.

He picked up the folder and glanced at the names of Lilou's parents, Félix and Nannette Basso. He'd made a personal visit, of course, to inform them of their daughter's death but he needed to properly interview them. Neither had reacted in what Luc would call a normal fashion. No tears, no surprises, not even relief. Monsieur Basso had cursed Luc, and Lilou's mother had simply poured herself another beer at the kitchen table.

Luc dragged a hand across his face in a sudden wave of exhaustion. Perhaps he could put Eloise on the case?

His field desk phone rang and it made him jump. It hadn't taken long—just three days of no televisions noise, no phones ringing, no bells or low-grade humming—to find himself acclimating to a much quieter world.

He picked up the phone, hoping it was Aix with a status on the vehicles.

"Luc DeBray," he said into the receiver. He listened quietly for a few moments and then replaced the phone receiver.

The vehicles would be delayed. Perhaps indefinitely. DeBray should attempt to make other arrangements.

He stood and walked to his door where he could see Madame Gabin pecking away at a manual typewriter. It was her own, which didn't surprise Luc. She'd always struggled with the word processor in the office anyway.

Three people sat in the waiting room. None of them looked to be in a terrible hurry. No bleeding parts, no real agitation. But the day was young. If it was anything like yesterday, bedlam was in the offing.

He signaled to the person closest to him, an elderly man who sat on a chair with his hat in his lap and his eyes trained on Luc.

"Monsieur Ayoub?" Luc said, motioning him into his office.

"It's about time," Monsieur Ayoub said as he got up. Behind him the door to the police station flew open and six people squeezed through, all arguing and speaking loudly. One of them was bleeding from the mouth.

"I am sorry, Monsieur Ayoub," Luc said, holding up a hand to stop him. "I must triage this situation first."

Cursing under his breath, Monsieur Ayoub took his seat again and eyed the newcomers with open resentment.

"Everybody calm down!" Luc said to the room. "I'll take you one at a time."

As he returned to his office with the bleeding man, his eye fell on Lilou's folder and he felt a sliver of regret.

Not yet, *ma petite*, he thought sorrowfully. *You must be patient.*

❈ ❈ ❈ ❈ ❈

Notre Mort was the ancient green moss covered non-working fountain two streets over from the Café Sucre where I'd first met Luc. It was where I was meeting Guy.

He was already there when I arrived so I got the chance to see how tall he was in relation to the huge fountain and the odd Grecian column. Guy had a slightly scruffy look to him but then so did most of the Frenchmen I'd seen in Chabanel—DeBray included.

I waved to him and when I approached he kissed me on both cheeks. I'm pretty sure both of mine were burning by the time he released me but he didn't seem to notice.

"*Bonjour, Jules*," he said, reminding me once more of how gorgeous my name sounds in French. Or maybe how surprisingly much phlegm is required to say it in certain cultures.

"*Bonjour, Guy*," I said, wondering how bad his English really was because he was about to discover how nonexistent my French was.

"Thank you so much for your help," I said in French and immediately congratulated myself until he answered with a string of gobble-de-gook that made me blanch.

This is the problem with attempting to speak someone else's language when you don't really know it. They think it means you understand them instead of realizing you only know two or three memorized phrases and if you go off script even a little you're totally lost.

"No *comprendo*," I said, lapsing into high school Spanish.

He laughed. "*Pas de problème*," he said, as he led me away from the fountain and down one of the streets. "We will speak slow, *oui*?"

Like that'll help, I thought, but I smiled encouragingly because he really seemed to think it might work.

"Wasn't it terrible about the girl Lilou?" I said.

"It is being so bad," he said.

"Do you know Hugo very well?"

He looked at me in surprise. "Hugo Remet?"

"I don't know his last name. The guy who lives in the apartment building."

"*Oui*, that is Hugo." He frowned. "He has had a hard life, yes? The drinking and I think prison."

Why doesn't that surprise me?

"A good man, though, I think," Guy said firmly.

Oh sure. With the drinking and the prison I'd already figured that.

"So you don't think he could have hurt Lilou?" I asked.

"Hugo? *Non. Ce n'est pas possible.*"

Yes, well, I'm sure that's what all of Jeffrey Dahmer's buddies said about him too.

I could tell my question had gotten Guy thinking but our language barrier was too much to get into the subject very deeply. He was likely worried about his sister living right next door to a potential serial killer. (I'd mentally filled in some of the gaps in Hugo's crime résumé in the time I'd had to think about it.)

The neighborhood of Guy's friend was on the further side of the village from the Poupard's place. From the *Notre Mort* fountain we walked down a long narrow road—are there any other kind in this village?—and then an alley. Most of the buildings in Chabanel were made of limestone and their colors varied from lemony yellow to ochre and every shade in between.

Even though Chabanel is a tiny village of no real consequence many of its older buildings have tall front columns and massive carved wooden doors with iron knockers featuring the faces of lions or bulldogs.

Once we came out of the alley, there was a wider cobblestoned street with a pizzeria and some kind of pharmacy shop. There didn't seem to be any rhyme or reason for why a certain shop or business was where it was. And the villagers lived on top of it all. There was no commercial district. It was all residential and commercial mushed together.

As we stood on the threshold buzzing to get entrance into Guy's friend's apartment, I began to focus on the purpose of our visit—something I'd been too preoccupied to do before now.

What would I do if it wasn't just France impaired by the EMP? What would I do if there was no USA to come home to? The thought wouldn't gel but by the way the goose bumps raced up and down my arm clearly it had on some level.

When Thibault buzzed us in, we stepped into a stairwell that was icy cold in spite of the warm weather outside. Not unlike the apartment building where I was currently living, this one had a very tiny elevator—now useless. I could see the cage that protected it from the cables and pulleys had been pried open and I wondered if someone had been trapped in there when the EMP went off.

We walked the four flights to Thibault's apartment and again I was reminded of how aerobic this apocalypse was going to be for those of us with a little extra weight to lose.

Guy didn't even have a chance to knock on the door before it was pulled open.

If I had to describe Thibault in one sentence I'd say he was the spitting image of Hugo's ugly brother. He was tall and greasy and wore straight-legged jeans with a dirty t-shirt. He had a sort of beard, full in some spots, sparse in most others. But his eyes were probing and sharp. They went first to my chest and then reluctantly to my face.

I disliked him from the get-go.

After we all exchanged greetings which thank God involved no kissing, Thibault ushered us into his living room where there was a series of lawn chairs and a long table piled high with what looked like junk electronics.

The one good thing about Thibault that I immediately discovered which tended to block out a lot of the bad was the fact that he spoke English.

Guy settled onto a couch to poke through a coffee table also full of junk in order to allow me to sit next to Thibault and his ham radio which turned out really to be just a big walkie talkie looking thing.

I edged as far away from Thibault as I could while still being able to hear and see what he was doing.

For nearly the whole walk over here when I wasn't thinking of Hugo killing all the neighborhood girls in Chabanel I was tamping down the excitement that I was about to find out the extent of the EMP situation in Atlanta. I thought about the Poupards in my apartment in Atlanta. I couldn't help but imagine how fearful they must be if there was anything similar going on in the US.

I hoped my neighbors would reach out to them but knowing them, they'd probably reach out in the process of stripping my condo.

Walking around Chabanel today had helped soothe my fears of the night before. While it was true we didn't have electricity in Chabanel—at least for now—it was also true that there didn't seem to be that big of a difference between Chabanel *before* the EMP and Chabanel *after* the EMP.

Except for no cell phones or working cash registers, life seemed to be pretty much the same, maybe even a little bit sweeter.

Without any other attempt at conversation, Thibault donned his headset and fiddled with the dials on the radio. I don't know what I was expecting but it stood to reason that ham radios would have gotten smaller since the days when they looked like giant technological wonders in some weirdo's garage or basement.

Thibault had an antenna on the roof attached to his battery-operated hand-held transceiver that he said could both transmit and receive just by changing frequencies.

I glanced at Guy at one point and he gave me a thumbs up. I felt a flood of gratitude to have friends—people who cared about me. Amazingly.

I sat with my hands in my lap, my basket of fish and cheese and bread at my feet, and listened to the sounds of the birds outside Thibault's balcony. There wasn't another sound—not a clock ticking or water gurgling in pipes—to break the stillness of the afternoon.

"Hello, N2ASD," Thibault said into his transmitter. "This is Aix234. I read you. How is it in Chicago today?"

I literally felt my insides freeze at his words. I studied his face to see if I could get a sense of what the ham operator on the other end was telling him. When Thibault glanced at me, he flicked a switch on his receiver and a young man's voice filled the salon.

"Real bad, dude," he said. "I don't know how much longer I'll be able to continue doing this. Does the rest of the world know what happened? I mean, this sucks. It really sucks."

"Roger, N2ASD," Thibault said. "The world knows. We in France are also hit. Who else have you talked to?"

The young man came back on. "I talked to New Zealand this morning. They're cool. No problems. But Germany is toast."

Thibault looked at me and frowned. "Toast?"

I shook my head helplessly. "Like us, I think," I said.

"Aix234, you still there?" the boy said.

"*Oui*, Chicago. I am here."

"Please tell someone to come help us. We've got no power, no water and there's no cops."

"*Mon Dieu*," Thibault said under his breath.

A few minutes later, after assuring the man in Chicago that he would tell the authorities, Thibault signed off and turned to me.

"I am sorry," he said. "It is much worse there than here."

I didn't even trust myself to speak and I must have looked like I was about to pass out because Guy jumped up and got me a glass of water. After a moment, I turned to Thibault.

"Have you talked with anyone else in the States?"

He nodded. "It is the same in many other places. Riots, no police. It appears a series of EMPs were set off near several US cities. Some cities still have infrastructure but most do not."

"The National Guard?"

"I do not know."

I looked out the balcony and saw the blue skies and the puffy clouds scuttling across it as if there wasn't a care for anyone to have. My eyes fell on the basket at my feet. On impulse, I pulled out the packet of fish and handed it to Thibault.

"*Merci*," I said, realizing I had just done the first of what I was sure would be many more occasions of bartering for the things I needed in this new life.

He nodded and took the fish.

"*Je suis désolé*," he said.

Susan Kiernan-Lewis

13

The Hard Way Back

A part of me wasn't even surprised.

I mean, after all, my country is a country of cowboys, rebels and loners. We believe in the individual, in vigilante justice, in getting and keeping what's ours.

In the right to bear arms.

If what had happened in France truly had happened in the US then I wasn't at all surprised that instead of produce markets and cafés with fresh-baked bread, there was looting and lawlessness.

Guy must have figured I was totally gob-smacked by it all because he walked me all the way back to the apartment to make sure I got there safely. A good thing too, since I have no memory of the walk, only images in my head of CeCe huddled in her condo with no lights, no weapons and only last weekend's left-over Chinese in a now darkened fridge.

I thought of the Poupards too of course and while I liked to make out that my neighbors were all selfish misanthropes, I had to believe that when push came to shove, they would pitch in and help the hapless foreigners who now had to figure out not only how to run Jules Hooker's finicky microwave but also how to survive in a city with no food markets except the Whole Foods on Peachtree Street which had probably already been looted.

I was all the way up the stairwell of my apartment with Guy holding my elbow the whole way—presumably so I didn't plunge to my death either because it was dark or I was suicidal—before I shook myself out of my black thoughts.

I unlocked my door and stood staring into the apartment. It was early evening now and with no moon, it was dark inside. The cat shot out and began winding around my legs and mewing.

"You are being okay now, Jules?" Guy said, his face a visage of worry.

"Yes, I'm fine. Thank you, Guy."

"Is...very much to think about."

"Yes, a lot to take in." I hesitated in the hallway, resisting for some reason going into the darkened apartment.

"You have the lights?" he said, gently pulling me into the apartment.

I stood in the small foyer as I listened to him rummage around the kitchen. When he returned he had a lit candle in one hand and a flashlight in the other.

The apartment looked a whole lot less bleak with him and his lighting in it.

I still clutched the basket of cheese and what was left of the baguette and on impulse I turned to him and shoved it into his arms.

"Can you take this to the...old ladies?" I asked. The last thing I felt like doing was eat and I had no idea if the old dears had gone out today.

"*Oui*," he said, smiling sadly at me. "*Bien sûr.*"

I can't really account for the rest of the night. I know I found a bit of cheese for the cat and miraculously found two glasses left of the wine that Guy had brought over the night before.

I knew it wouldn't help anything—least of all those poor people back in the States—and certainly not me and my situation here, but I couldn't stop thinking about what I'd learned from Thibault and his ham radio. I couldn't stop hearing that young man's voice.

As I sat in the salon watching the candle sputter to its end and drinking the wine, I made sure that I faced the fact that if it was true and the infrastructure of the US had collapsed and there was no country for me to go home to then I had to start thinking about what I would do with my life here in France.

I didn't know yet what that meant or how that looked and as I finished off the last of the wine, I allowed myself the luxury of not trying to figure it out tonight.

I said a prayer for CeCe and for Gilbert—and my mother in Canada—and then I stumbled the six yards from the living room to the bedroom where I collapsed, only vaguely aware that the cat had jumped on the bed and had settled down around my hip.

The first official day of the new world order was done.

And so was the life I'd known up to then.

14

The Real Work Begins

The next morning I woke up feeling like crap. Not mentally since, amazingly, the sun was shining through my bedroom window providing me with a luscious view of a perfect south of France day, but physically because my mouth was dry, my make up was sticking to my cheeks and the flirty Miu Miu skirt that I'd found on sale at Lenox Square a week before my trip looked like somebody had used it to buff a car.

That was not hyperbole since I knew I would never be able to iron the pleats back into the skirt and could only conjure up images of Wilma Flintstone heating up the shell of a turtle to iron Fred's shirts.

By the time I washed up, finished off the last of the cheese and apricots in the fridge and dressed for the day—in a knock-off Louis Vuitton corset over cropped cotton slacks—I felt better and had some semblance of a plan.

My intention to find out what happened to Lilou had gotten briefly derailed by my unanticipated obsession with my own predicament. I reminded myself that I could do nothing for anybody back in the States and I wasn't exactly sure what I could even do for myself with the new world order.

But I could focus on my commitment to do what Luc didn't have time to do.

I could at least do that.

Locking my apartment, I kept an ear open for the old ladies but their apartment was quiet. *They must be late risers*, I decided as I walked to Merci's apartment down the hall and knocked. I wasn't really sure what Merci did for a living—at least before the EMP—but whatever it was she didn't seem to do it until late afternoon.

There was a note tacked to Merci's door and I pulled it off and knocked. When Merci answered, a toothbrush in her mouth and surprise in her eyes, I handed her the note.

"Special delivery," I said. "Are you busy today?"

"*Bonjour*, Jules," she said around her toothbrush as she took the note. I couldn't help noticing that the note was signed *Maman*.

"You look amazing," Merci said of my outfit. "Are you okay? Guy told me about last night."

"I'm better," I said briskly. "I was wondering if I could steal you for the morning?"

"Steal me?" She frowned and I guessed I'd hit on one of the few idioms she didn't know.

"I wanted to ask our neighbors some questions about what they might have seen the day Lilou was killed."

Merci held up a finger and then ran to the kitchen to spit out her toothpaste. She turned back and grinned.

"You are investigating it, yes?"

"The cops don't have time, so yeah, I thought I would."

"*Bon*," she said, rummaging for something in a drawer in the small dining room. "I am writing a quick note to *ma mere* and then we will be off."

"Are you sure? I don't want to interrupt something you were supposed to be doing with your mom."

"My *mom*, as you say, will be delighted to see I have a new friend," Merci said with a laugh. "She and I can always get together." She wrote a quick message on the back of the note and thumbtacked it to the outside of her apartment door before shutting it behind her.

It was pretty clear that I'd better start saving my notepaper. This business of passing notes via thumbtacks was obviously going to be our new email system going forward.

"But first I have to talk with a friend. Can we meet by *Notre Mort*?"

"That'd be great, Merci."

Deciding this meant I had time to grab a croissant at the nearby *patisserie*, I walked downstairs with Merci before we split ways.

"A *bientôt*!" she said.

"And to you," I said, figuring that was some form of goodbye. *See? I'm learning French by osmosis!*

Minelli's *patisserie*—which I'm learning is not the same as a *boulangerie*—was on the corner of my street and directly across from the Café Sucre.

I have to say I love the experience of stepping into either of the two bakeries in Chabanel. The sugary delights on display are equally delightful by their fragrance—all vanilla and sweetness. And that's before you even get to the tasting part!

But the *patisserie* was something special. First the windows are amazing—three shelves of plump cream cakes, fruit tarts, *pains au chocolat*, *profiteroles*, *chou à la crèmes*, *éclairs au chocolat,* mini-*flans*, *galettes,* and *mille-feuilles*—all to make you weep and every single one of them a work of art.

I couldn't imagine who got up and created all these— or that there were really enough people in Chabanel to gobble them up every single day. But clearly there were. Because every day the shelves were full and every night only crumbs were left.

Even so, I was surprised to see how busy *Minelli's* was. There were three women inside—most of them looking to be my mother's age—and one very strikingly handsome American man.

"Jim!" I said as I moved toward him.

His face lit up with pleasure at seeing me. He kissed me on both cheeks and then stepped out of line to stand with me at the back of the line.

"Wow, that is quite the outfit," he said. "I was hoping I'd see you today."

"I'm sorry again about bailing on you after the town square meeting the other night," I said.

"No worries at all. How are you settling in with everything?" He waved a hand to encompass the *patisserie* but of course he meant the other thing—the end of the world thing.

"Okay, I guess. Have you heard what's happened back in the States?"

His face instantly fell and I hated that I'd brought it up. Things had been pleasant up to then. Almost normal.

"My sources say not good," he said. "Not good at all."

"Yeah, me too. Do you have people back home you're worried about?"

Dumb question because who besides me has nobody back home?

"Not really," he said with a shrug. "Both my folks are gone. I have an ex-wife but trust me, the bandits and opportunists should look out for *her*."

I laughed politely thinking this is probably the first of a whole new range of post-apocalyptic humor. Not sure it's ever going to be a favorite of mine.

"Any idea how you're going to pay for things now that the ATMs don't work and we can't access US banks?" I asked.

"I'm okay for awhile," he said as we inched forward in the line. "I've been talking with a guy named Esteban who runs the village newspaper. I'm talking to him about maybe letting me write some articles for him."

"They pay for that?"

"Not much," he admitted.

"Would you be writing in French or English?"

"A little bit of both. There's a fairly large ex-pat community in Aix."

Crap. I was going to end up having to babysit or wash windows to keep body and soul together.

"Did you hear about the murder on rue Gaston de Saporta?" I asked.

He sighed. "Yes. It's terrible. Did it have to do with the EMP?"

The murder wasn't discovered until after the EMP so the papers hadn't covered it because right at the moment the papers weren't covering squat.

"No," I said. "She was a mentally challenged girl named Lila Basso. Ever hear of her?"

He shook his head. "No, but Chabanel has over five thousand people. I tend to know more Anglos than French. And most of those live in Aix."

"How did you hear about the murder?"

"The police scanners," he said, looking at the display case of pastries before us. "One of our ex-pat members is obsessed with following them and he mentioned it to me. I mean, murder is a big deal in Chabanel because it doesn't happen."

"What did your friend hear the cops say on the scanner about it?" I still didn't even know how Lilou died; kind of a serious roadblock to my investigation. How can I look for a murder weapon when I don't know what to look for?

Jim frowned as if in thought.

"Something about they found her bike by an old watchman's shed near the canal?"

I felt a surge of excitement. A clue! A real live honest-to-God clue!

"Really? The cops think Lilou rode her bike to the canal? Do they think she was killed there?"

"I really don't know, Jules," Jim said with a small smile. "But I do know that *you* should be the one writing for the paper here, not me. You're a real Lois Lane. Would you be interested? I could talk to Esteban."

"That would be great, Jim, thanks. Meanwhile I'll get busy learning to write in fluent French."

He laughed. "Well, it's not like you have anything else to do."

❊❊❊❊❊❊

After making a date with Jim to meet for coffee later in the week, I hurried to the fountain to meet Merci. When I approached she was talking to a thin young man about her own age. When she spied me, she quickly kissed the guy and turned to me, all blushes and smiles.

"Is that your boyfriend?" I asked as the young man disappeared around the corner.

"Pfutt!" Merci said with a laugh. "I have known Gerard since we were children. He was asking if I knew about the black market on the rue de Carmes. He was going there to get *foie gras*."

Only in France would *foie gras* still be a thing after the big one drops, I thought. Then I wondered if I should be going there myself or at least asking some French-speaking person to go and buy stuff for me.

"Do they take money?" I asked.

"They take anything," Merci said with a smile and a raised eyebrow.

Wow. So post-apocalyptic prostitution was already happening. Oh, well, I decided not knock it until I was completely sure it wouldn't end up being my back up plan.

God, I hope that's just a joke.

Merci threaded her arm through mine and we turned back toward our neighborhood where we proceeded to spend the entire morning knocking on doors so that Merci could ask the single question: *Did you see Lilou the day she was killed?*

Unfortunately, no matter how long Merci ended up talking to the neighbors—and some of them were quite long-winded—it turned out that not a single person had seen Lilou. Since I now knew she was not on a bicycle when she was in our neighborhood, if someone said they'd seen Lilou in the area and she was on her bike, I knew that they must be remembering another day.

Most of the neighbors up and down the street were very curious about me. When Merci explained to them who I was—I was able to pick out *Americaine* and *tant pis* and a whole lot of head-shaking in their conversation—I realized that I was at least as of much interest to everyone as the dead girl.

I also picked up on a good bit of hostility. I'd prepared myself for that and cursed myself for not telling Merci beforehand to tell everyone I was Canadian.

We finished the last house just before noon. Knowing how vitally important the lunch hour was to every French person I'd met so far I assumed Merci would want to chow down somewhere and was relieved to hear she was willing to miss a meal for my sake.

It's possible she might have been thinking of saving her food for later. Regardless of what Mayor Beaufait had said, life without electricity and transportation was anything but business as usual no matter how hard everyone might want it to appear so.

Merci glanced at her watch.

"I have time for one more translation, Jules," she said. "But then I must meet my mother to plan Sunday lunch."

To let you know how important Sunday lunch was to the French: today was Friday.

Two days after an apocalyptic event.

"I think we've canvassed everyone in the neighborhood," I said. "Do you think it would be possible to talk with Lilou's parents?"

Merci hesitated and I didn't blame her. Talking to recently bereaved parents would make the strongest of us balk.

"I...really?" she asked with a frown. "Is that a good idea?"

"Well, it won't be fun. But yeah. If you know where they live, it would be a big help."

"You don't think the police will have interviewed them?"

"Beyond telling them the bad news? My guess is no. Please, Merci? Just fifteen minutes and then you're free to go. I promise."

She gnawed a fingernail and glanced down the street before letting out a long sigh.

"Okay," she said. "But please to remember this was your idea."

It appeared that the Bassos lived on the outskirts of the village and if Chabanel had a section of town that was, as we Americans call it, *the wrong side of the tracks*, then well, *voila* the Basso homestead.

I'd already started to feel uncomfortable the further we walked away from the main hub of things, but Merci didn't seem too concerned. There were a few seedy characters loitering along the sidewalk as fewer and fewer shops gave way to no shops or ones that had obviously been boarded up long before the EMP dropped.

I knew that Lilou Basso was mentally challenged but now I knew she was poor too. That made her the perfect victim for most predators and certainly ideal for the needs of the classic serial killer.

As we walked, Merci filled me in on what she knew about Lilou's family and I honestly wished she'd told me before we were a half a block away because I'm pretty sure I would've said *on second thought*...

Apparently Lilou's mother Nannette used to be the village prostitute or whatever the French version of that is, and her father Felix lived in a constant state of defensiveness as a result. *Violent and unpredictable* is the way Merci put it. In any case she warned me not to expect either of them to act like normal parents under the circumstances and now I *really* wanted to turn back.

By the time we were walking up to the very battered and peeling door of 142 rue de Mégisseries, I was sure this was a seriously bad idea.

"What do you want me to ask?" Merci asked as she held her fist poised over the door, ready to knock.

"First tell them how sorry we are about what happened," I said, really not liking our being here one bit and now realizing that Luc DeBray would probably not like it either. Not that that mattered.

"Of course. And after that?" Merci asked as she proceeded to knock on the door.

"Ask what Lilou intended to do that day," I said hurriedly as footsteps sounded from inside.

When the door swung open it was all I could do not to recoil and take a step backward, or let's face it, run in the opposite direction at triple speed.

Nannette Basso opened the door like she expected the devil himself to be there—and she was determined to out-evil him. Her face was ravaged with wrinkles and scars. One eye drooped, revealing a milky blue eyeball, yet both eyes were still outlined in kohl and slathered with clotted mascara. The effect was a drag queen dressed for Halloween.

Madame Basso squinted at us on her door step and then barked out something that I had no hope of understanding. I prayed that Merci wasn't as mesmerized by the sight of Nannette Basso as I was because otherwise we'd be standing on her doorstep all afternoon.

Merci responded quickly and by the slight softening of Nannette's face—and by softening I definitely mean drooping—I could tell that Merci was extending our condolences.

Nanette's response was sharp and cold.

And for some reason, her eyes were on me.

And only me.

For the next sixty seconds during which Merci rapidly presented her question about Lilou's whereabouts on her last day, Nanette never stopped staring at me—not even when she needed to make the necessary effort to curl her lip, revealing very brown and crooked teeth.

I can't remember whether I tried to smile to disarm her or whether I thought she might think that was inappropriate. I can't remember what my face was doing beyond being frozen in horror.

In any case, eventually Nannette spewed out a fairly lengthy answer to Merci before giving me one last *you make me want to vomit* look (hey turns out I do understand nonverbal French!) and slamming the door.

When she did, I realized I'd been holding my breath. Merci and I both turned and nearly ran to the first corner which lead back to the village.

"What was that all about? She looked pretty angry. She doesn't think *we* killed Lilou, does she? Because that's kind of what it felt like."

"Well, yes and no, as you Americans say," Merci said as we scurried past the same group of n'er-do-wells who'd body-searched us with their eyeballs on the way there.

I have to admit to feeling very nervous as we passed them and was reminded once more that assault and battery would not rank high on Luc DeBray's list of things to attend to today. Not with all the other chores he'd be dealing with thanks to the EMP.

"So what did she say?" I asked as we left the sinister gang behind.

"She said Lilou did what she did every day. She took her bike to school where she checked in and then ditched class to go into Chabanel."

"Her mother knew that Lilou ditched school every day?"

Merci nodded.

"And then what did she do?"

"Madame Basso didn't really know everything that Lilou got up to in her day but she said Lilou always returned home by seven o'clock for dinner. Three nights ago she didn't."

"Did she call the cops?"

"No, because she said Lilou had done this before once or twice but had always turned up."

"And she didn't worry about her?"

"Obviously not," Merci said with a sad shrug.

"Why did she keep staring at me like *I* was the murderer?"

Merci sighed. "She is a crazy old woman made crazier by her daughter's murder, Jules."

"Okay, but why was she staring at me like that?"

"She has a theory about who killed Lilou and the police haven't returned her calls to hear it."

"The cops haven't interviewed her?" *I knew it!*

"She said not."

"What's her theory and why do I get the feeling it has something to do with me?"

"Not you. America."

"Now I am totally confused."

"She said there was a man she'd seen with Lilou. Someone she wasn't supposed to be with."

I felt the sweat begin to bead up on my forehead the moment Merci said that. Some how I think I knew what she was going to say.

"I guess she was staring at you like that," Merci said as she tucked my hand onto her arm and guided me along, "because she sort of blames the US for what happened to Lilou."

I cleared my throat but it wasn't very effective.

"The guy she saw with Lilou was American?" I asked.

Merci nodded. "A big guy. Named Jim Anderson."

15

Objects May Be Closer Than They Appear

Even though I am in every other respect the quintessential Southern girl I don't think I'm often given to such stereotypical proclivities as the vapors but I have to admit to feeling a tad woozy when Merci mentioned Jim Anderson's name.

Merci must have seen it because she led me to the first café table we came to.

Thank God for café tables that literally exist every few steps in this town. I seriously have no idea how I've managed to survive without them up to now.

As soon as my legs collapsed beneath me and I sank into the chair, the waiter was there and instead of staring at me as if he had no idea why I was there—as he'd done every other time I'd gone to a café—Merci burbled off some French and he was back in a flash with a tot of brandy and a little cookie thing.

I threw the brandy back and took in a long breath.

There had to be a perfectly reasonable explanation for why Lilou's mother thought Jim knew her daughter. And after that there then must be another perfectly reasonable explanation for why Jim claimed not to know Lilou. Granted that was a lot of perfectly reasonable explanations. But I was optimistic.

Merci was watching me with undisguised concern and perhaps a little horror. I asked her to order me another brandy—and herself too—and then made a serious attempt to Get. A. Grip.

"I know an American here in Chabanel named Jim Anderson," I said.

Merci's eyebrows shot up. "You do?"

I nodded. "I asked him just today if he knew Lilou Basso and he said no."

Merci frowned. "So he's lying?"

"Well, that's one way to look at it. Or perhaps it's a case of mistaken identity? The mother didn't look too credible to me."

"She wasn't drunk," Merci pointed out.

"No, but she was distraught," I countered.

"Was she? I mean she was annoyed that the cops had not called her back but I didn't sense that she was...overly upset in any way. Did you? Oh! There is *Maman*!" Merci waved to a middle-aged woman who was walking down the sidewalk, a market basket on her arm.

Merci introduced her mother—who actually spoke a little English—before the two set off together to plan the Incredibly Important Sunday Lunch and left me at the table to pull myself together in my own time.

The waiter came back with the two brandies and looked at me as if he'd been suckered in some way now that he had to deal with just me. I looked at the bill he'd placed down with the drinks and quickly provided the euros to cover it which seemed to mitigate his bad mood a little.

I sat there and drank both brandies and felt the world a lot warmer and happier place in no time.

Of course this was a case of mistaken identity. It had to be. There was no other explanation for it. Well, there was but not one I was willing to address just yet. Not when I was finally feeling so relaxed and fuzzy about life in the apocalypse.

Jim had been nothing but kind to me from the moment we'd met. I have to say I have a pretty good sense about people—except for that time I dated a guy for three months before realizing he did a drag performance every Friday night at Atlanta's famous Red Door in Midtown. But in my defense he was a *very* good actor and so my naiveté was really more a testimony to Bobbi (okay yes in hindsight I can see there were signs) and his superior acting skills than my gullibility.

Anyway, I decided to give Jim the benefit of the doubt. It was the least I could do for a fellow American.

Innocent until proven guilty, right? I don't know if that's a thing over here but they could certainly learn from it if it isn't. In the spirit of the pursuit of justice and the American way (I was really feeling a little high about now) I decided that Jim simply could not be a suspect—not while I liked him so much. And that was that.

Which suddenly reminded me of the tip that Jim had given me at the *patisserie*. Determined to go forward with any and all clues that I uncovered—and realizing that there was no way Jim would give me important information about the murder if he was the murderer—I paid my brandy tab and on only slightly unsteady legs got up to go looking for directions to the nearest canal.

❖❖❖❖❖

Eloise and Matteo stood in Luc's office. Luc noticed that Eloise was close to tears and she was not a woman given to tears. They were all overwhelmed. They were all daily attempting to plug holes in a dripping colander.

"I told them I had no answers for when the lights would come on," Eloise said, her bottom lip trembling.

"Keep telling them that," Luc said tiredly. "I will meet with the mayor's office again later today to see about getting more lanterns and more fuel."

"That won't turn on their laptops," Matteo said drily.

Matteo was Luc's second-in-command. Fat, with his shirt tail usually half way out of his trousers and a permanent sneer on his lips, Matteo seriously annoyed Luc who always felt as if Matteo was second-guessing him or talking behind his back in an attempt to discredit his authority.

Even so, Luc knew his feelings toward Matteo weren't professional or acceptable.

"No and the sooner they realize that the sooner we can stop indulging these minor grievances," Luc said firmly. "If they don't have a crime to report, if they are not bleeding—"

"Yes, Chief," Matteo said. "We know. Placate them and move on."

"There's nothing else we can do at this point," Luc said but he was talking to Eloise. "As long as they have food and shelter, and no crime has been committed, the rest is simply inconvenience."

"Unless they're hurt or sick," Matteo said.

"Yes, Matteo, didn't I just say that?" Luc said briskly. "If they're bleeding and can't be treated here in Chabanel, they're to be transported to the hospital in Aix."

Luc glanced out his window and saw the American woman Jules Hooker hurrying by. He frowned. She knew nobody in town. He should send Eloise over to check on her later.

"We'll need more petrol," Matteo said. "When is it coming?"

It struck Luc that Matteo was starting to be nearly as difficult as the people who came pounding on his door asking if he had a spare flashlight.

"The petrol is coming when Aix delivers it," Luc said flatly. "Meanwhile, take your beat on foot tonight, Matteo. It won't hurt to get a little closer to the people. Eloise, take the car. There are two farms—the Durands and the Augustins—that nobody's heard from. Stop in and make sure they're all right."

Eloise nodded and gave her jacket a tug as if to straighten herself up too.

"What about the Lilou Basso case?" she asked quietly.

Luc dismissed them both with a wave.

"Let's take care of the living right now, shall we?" he said sternly.

He could have sworn he heard Matteo make a snorting sound but it was too subtle to qualify as insubordination.

Besides what if it had? He needed the man.

God knows, now more than ever.

✸✸✸✸✸✸

I have never stolen anything my life. This is especially true if work office supplies don't count. As I was looking at the bicycle propped up by one of the bakeries without any lock or chain on it I couldn't help but think that the owner must have at least on some level wanted the bike to be taken.

That makes total sense, doesn't it? Why else just display it on the street? The sign saying *Please Take My Bike* must have fallen off but in every other respect I was sure I was getting the full picture.

Proud of myself for locating the canal on a city kiosk map in lieu of doing it on my iPhone—which of course I don't have any more—I realized that where I needed to go was not comfortably accessible on foot.

So *voila* here I am staring at someone else's unlocked, unwatched bike.

Even though I have no experience with theft I have to say I think I'm a fairly good observer of human behavior which is all I have to say in my defense for why I was able to walk over to the bike—without looking around in any sort of a guilty manner—hop onto it and ride away as if it were my own. If stopped I was fully prepared to say that the bike was the spitting image of mine and since I never lie I had high hopes of that fact being evident on my face.

In any case, nobody stopped me.

Seeing the village from a bike is a whole different reality from seeing it on foot or even in a car. For one thing, you have total control of where you're going on a bike and if you ever saw the narrow weird alleys and streets in Chabanel you'd know what I mean.

Half the passageways for vehicular traffic are impassible either because they're too narrow or because they have these weird cement columns that abruptly emerge from the ground at no set time, rhyme or reason in order to bar vehicles from entering.

So, yeah, I was liking the bike.

In the back of my mind was the idea that I should probably ride the bike from Lilou's neighborhood to trace the route to her school and then to the garden at the back of my apartment. I still didn't know for sure if that's where she met her end so I was just going on the info I had. But even on a bike I wasn't thrilled at the thought of returning to Lilou's neighborhood any time soon.

Did I mention what a pleasant ride it was? Yes, it was bumpy as hell with the whole cobblestone thing but this vantage point gave me a unique view of life in Chabanel two days after the EMP.

Mayor Beaufait must be pleased.

The bakeries were open as were the bars and the cafés I passed. June was high tourist season in Aix which wasn't that far away so I figured there could be a few Brits and

Americans trapped here same as me. Maybe not in Chabanel but in other outlying villages. I had the idea I might swing by some of the hotels in Aix in a few days to see if anybody wanted to make friends. On the other hand, I'd already picked up the feeling that most of the French people I met blamed me specifically and all Americans in general for what had happened to them.

Maybe going to the hotels where all the Americans were hanging out right now wasn't my best idea.

It didn't take long to break free of the neighborhoods and streets of the center of the village. Not surprisingly, the further I got from the town hall roundabout at the heart of Chabanel the less populated the streets became. Fortunately, I wasn't going into the warehouse district which was nearer to Lilou's neighborhood and when I passed the sign for *Mégisseries* I knew the canal couldn't be far. Merci had told me *Mégisseries* mean tanneries so I'm guessing this was the bad side of town even in the eighteen hundreds.

The weather was glorious today with fluffy white clouds drifting across an intensely blue sky. I tried to imagine Van Gogh or Cezanne using this light to make their famous paintings. It was a lot easier than trying to imagine some terrorist fashioning a dirty bomb and igniting it over the Mediterranean. How could anyone possibly look at this beautiful sky and think *let's mess this up?*

I shook myself out of these thoughts right about the time I saw that on the other side of the last of the buildings a highway ran left and right through the countryside. That had to mean the canal was near and sure enough, once I crossed the vacant highway I could see it.

It was smaller than I thought it would be, just a grassy canal with ancient oxen paths along the sides. God knows how long it had been used to bring goods to Chabanel. Centuries probably.

What had drawn Lilou to this place? I wondered as I stopped my bike and gazed out over the scene. It was lovely in a lonely sort of way. I wasn't sure how different it was now that the EMP had thrown everyone back to the eighteen hundreds. Would there have been much activity on the canal or the towpath when Lilou was here four days ago?

It was easy to spot the watchman's shed that Jim had mentioned. The little building was the only structure anywhere near the canal. It was tiny and I couldn't imagine what it might have been used for. Storage maybe? I dropped my bike in the grass and walked toward it.

As I got closer I could see that the roof was half caved in and that a slab of cement formed a sort of porch in front. I tried the handle on the door and wasn't surprised to see it was locked.

To tell you the truth I wasn't all that disappointed about that. With the roof open to the elements, God knows what would be inside. Looking in was one thing, going in and rummaging around was quite another, thank you. Especially since I was wearing my faux Vuitton corset. Perfect for biking in the south of France on a summer day: less so for exploring dirty rat-infested sheds.

The small shed was built onto a concrete slab that jutted out over the canal. There were small rectangular windows on one side. I could have stood on the ground and looked through the closest window except it was covered by a tangled vine of honeysuckle that crawled the wall and over the roof's edge. I wondered if France had water moccasins that hung out near water the way they did in Georgia. I decided not to trust the bush which could easily hide an entire family reunion of water moccasins.

The second nearest window was actually above the water and the only way I was going to look through it was to slide sideways on the tips of my ballet flats along the concrete ledge that ran along the bottom of the shed wall.

Was seeing inside that important?

Why else had I stolen a bicycle and come all this way? I scolded myself. It would probably reveal nothing—since the cops knew about it—but maybe I'd see something they missed.

As I stepped on the ledge and began moving slowly toward the second window, I have to admit I'd already pretty much consigned this whole venture to the *desperate to do something* column in my mind and was half-thinking about getting back to town to see if there were any almond croissants left at the bakery.

All of which is my excuse for why I didn't hear anything out of the ordinary the split second before I felt a terrible pressure in the middle of my back as a pair of unseen hands gave me a hard push.

I lost my grip and began to fall.

16

From the Bottom Up

The sensation of falling backwards is a very surreal feeling—especially when you didn't *intend* to go over backwards like scuba divers do when they jump off a boat. And knowing that *where* you were falling backwards into was a filthy and disease-ridden cesspool, well, let's just say that a long and hysterical scream accompanied my tumble into the canal.

Because oh yeah, make no mistake, I fell into the damn thing, knocking my head against the cement side and scraping my elbow on the way down.

By the time I hit the water—disgusting brackish stuff that went up my nose—I was already sure my assailant was going to finish me off with a fish gutting knife or maybe a bullet to the head.

I sputtered and splashed in the canal water, not at all sure I should be trying to climb out any where near the shed where the person who pushed me in might be waiting for me. But I saw no-one near the shed and as cold and freaked out as I was, I knew I needed to get out of the water more than I needed to worry about whoever it was who pushed me in.

I know that makes no sense and I've hesitated saying it up to now for that very reason but that's how I felt. It seems to me that there's a certain kind of woman—and clearly I am one—who would rather die than have amoebae and mud in her hair for longer than absolutely necessary.

I pulled myself up the bank and sat shivering and trying not to throw up while my eyes combed the area around the shed.

Even miserable—and trust me I was miserable—I couldn't turn off the part of my brain that was wondering if someone followed me or if this was just some lowlife looking for a hapless victim.

But why push someone into the canal if you didn't intend to rob them? And pushing someone into the canal pretty much negates the possibility of robbing them since, hello, they're in the canal!

Does this have anything to do with Lilou? I wondered. *Is this what happened to Lilou?* Even in the late June sun—which was quickly dropping—I was trembling so badly I was nearly convulsing. I got to my feet, praying that my attacker hadn't stolen my bike, and began to run.

❈❈❈❈❈

The good news is that I had my money and keys in my pocket so I was able to let myself into my apartment without breaking anything. The bad news was yeah, my stolen bike had been stolen again so it took me over an hour to trudge home, wet, tired and totally unnerved.

But that also gave me time to sort out what had happened.

Sort of.

I was so focused on how physically miserable I was—and let's face it there was no way any amount of scrubbing was going to get red mud out of the fabric on my totally ruined corset—that all I could think of was about that, oh, and wondering if someone was following me.

By the time I reached my apartment, I'd stripped off the parts of my outfit that weren't covering anything important and dropped them on the kitchen floor. My shower wasn't working of course, but I did have a large pail of water in the kitchen that Guy had brought over yesterday. He'd brought water to Mercy and the old ladies too.

I know the water was supposed to be for drinking or cooking but I couldn't bear the feeling of the canal water on me a minute longer and so I used it with dishwashing soap to wash the smell of my awful day from my skin and hair.

Once I was clean and in dry clothes I spent a few moments regretting that I had drunk what was left of the wine last night and wishing I'd made it to the bakeries before they closed.

I was in the middle of this crisis—still not completely processing what had happened to be today—when there was a knock at the door. Hoping it might be a pizza delivery guy who hadn't gotten word of the apocalypse, I opened it to find Luc DeBray in the hall.

"May we talk?" he said.

I couldn't help looking at his hands which held a bag with what looked like a bottle inside.

"Sure," I said.

"Is everything all right?" he asked, frowning at me.

I have to tell you I am not the kind of girl who busts out crying at the drop of a hat. It's true. If anything, I'm too tough. So I was as surprised as anyone when his question made me burst into tears. I don't know.

Probably the whole unresolved *someone tried to kill me* thing was starting to sink in.

"Jules, *essaie*," he said taking my elbow and then turning it to examine the fresh scrapes on it. He led me to the couch and made me sit down. Then he went to the kitchen and returned with wine glasses and a wine opener. He quickly opened the wine and poured two glasses.

"What happened?" he asked, nodding at the pile of wet clothes in the hallway.

What the hell, I thought. The worst he can do is arrest me and then he'll have to feed me three squares.

"I heard that Lilou Basso's bike was found at the watchman's shed by the canal," I said, tossing back a long gulp of the very nice rosé. "So I stole a bike and went to see for myself. At which point somebody pushed me in the canal."

Saying the words somehow made the whole situation even worse if that's at all possible and I was living it so trust me it is. The look on Luc's face, though, helped a great deal and in any other situation I'm sure I would have laughed.

I drained my wine glass and looked expectantly at the wine bottle.

"Pushed you in? Are you sure you didn't slip?"

God, does he think I don't know the difference? I thought with mounting anger.

Before I could answer, he said, "Why are you obsessed with Lilou Basso?"

I have to say I did not like him using the word *obsessed* one little bit. I thought it was definitely pointing the conversation in a certain *this American is crazy* kind of direction and the thought majorly annoyed me.

"I am not obsessed. I am *determined*," I said waving my empty wine glass at him, "to see justice for poor Lilou and you are too busy to investigate her murder yourself."

To Luc's credit he hesitated only a moment before refilling my glass.

I lost myself momentarily in the lovely wine, the feeling of warmth it was giving me—that and the dry clothes—and the comfort of having a handsome man in my living room.

"It is true," he said slowly, "that we are very busy now."

I wondered how it was he had time to check on me with a bottle of wine if he was that busy but I certainly didn't want to bring it up. I liked having a cop in my living room. Especially this one.

He glanced out the balcony where Lilou's body had been found.

"Other things must wait," he said with a shrug.

I wanted to say *And then obviously get totally forgotten* but since I was drinking his wine I thought it wiser not to mention it.

"Can you at least tell me how she died?" I asked softly, afraid that any moment this detente between us would evaporate.

"Strangled. With hands, not a weapon or belt."

"So probably by a man."

He nodded.

"Sex?" I asked and very much hoped he didn't think I was making an offer.

He shook his head.

"Well, at least that," I said.

It occurred to me that in this spirit of sharing, I should tell him that I'd spoken to Lilou's mother—not to mention half the neighborhood—but I didn't want to ruin the pleasant exchange. Maybe that's also the reason I decided not to tell him what I'd heard about Jim Anderson.

Well, that and the fact that I didn't want to point the finger at Jim until I had more evidence. It had nothing to do with the fact that he was a fellow American. I was almost positive about that.

Luc stood up, effectively breaking the spell between us. "Will you be okay?" he said.

I nodded. "Thanks for checking on me. Thanks for this." I lifted my glass in a toast to him.

He smiled. "*De rien*," he said. "Lock your door behind me."

It wasn't until he'd gone that I realized he'd all but given me the green light to continue my investigation into Lilou's murder.

❊❊❊❊❊

That night as Neige and I attempted to get comfortable in bed, both of us hungry and restless, I realized for the first time how very alone I was here in France.

The fact that I hadn't heard from Mercy or the old ladies tonight—after three nights of camaraderie and food-sharing—made me realize that the bottom line was that I was an outsider to them too. They had no reason to trust me—especially considering I was a stranger and worse, an American.

Even Luc, as lovely as he could be, was so formal in so many ways. And regardless of how well he spoke English there was still plenty of room for misunderstanding between us.

I found myself wondering how to contact Jim and how comforting it would be hear his American accent about now.

You know. Unless it turns out he's a ruthless killer.

I punched the pillow—fruitless since my inability to sleep had nothing to do with how comfy my bed linens were or weren't—and couldn't help but do a head count of all the people who were in the *patisserie* this morning when Jim told me about the shed on the canal.

Except for a few middle-aged women whom I'd never seen before, Jim was the only one who knew I was going to be at the canal that afternoon.

Stop it! You're talking yourself into distrusting the one person in town who you really need as a friend!

Frustrated, I lay in bed listening to the muffled sounds of voices throughout the apartment building. I couldn't tell who or what they were saying but still wished I had the hum of a fan or air conditioner to drown them out.

I tried to distract myself by praying for CeCe's safety and for my mom and also my cat before I realized I hadn't prayed for Gilbert. I was tempted not to, frankly, thinking he could just fend for himself without my and God's help but in the end I threw a prayer in his direction too.

Moments later, I got up to make sure I'd put what was left of the wine in the fridge. Even though the refrigerator no longer worked, it still kept things cooler than sitting out on my coffee table. As I tiptoed into the living room using the flashlight to light my way, I immediately saw something that hadn't been there when I went to bed.

A stark white envelope was shoved halfway under the door.

Thinking this might be some kind of bizarre post-apocalyptic block party invitation, I picked it up and pulled a note out which read in English,

Leave Lilou alone or you are nect.

17

Only the Lonely

I held the note in my hand and tried to keep my heart from pounding out of my chest. At first I couldn't believe what I was reading but on the fourth read-through it was pretty clear. I finally staggered over to the couch where I sat down hard and looked at the door, wondering if I'd been too tired to lock it when I went to bed.

Not that it mattered now since obviously the letter-writer only wanted to warn me, not kill me.

At least not yet.

I re-read the note a fifth time and tried to understand what it meant. Whoever wrote it knew some English, in spite of the fact that the word *next* was misspelled.

It immediately occurred to me that as a native English speaker Jim would never have misspelled such an easy word. Did that mean he didn't send the note—and so for sure wasn't Lilou's killer?

Or was he smart enough to deliberately misspell the word to throw me off?

I ran a hand through my hair and put the note down, suddenly sickened even to be touching the same scrap of paper that Lilou's killer had touched.

Because one thing was for sure, the only reason anyone would want me to stop looking for Lilou's killer was because they didn't want to be found out and evidently *I was on the right track for doing exactly that.*

Is it someone I've talked to?

I looked at the front door again and this time I got up and double checked that it was locked.

Leave Lilou alone or you are nect.

Neige ran out of the bedroom and sat in the doorway looking at me indictingly. He gazed around the room before heading into the kitchen presumably in search of milk or kibble.

Sorry kitty.

Should I tell Luc about this? Except he's got so much on his plate already.

I picked up the note again but I couldn't tell if the handwriting was male or female, American, British or French. It was printed neatly with what looked like a ballpoint pen on a page whose tattered side showed that it had been ripped out of a spiral book

I couldn't help but think of Jim again. But wouldn't that have been too big a risk, coming to my apartment? He's very memorable. Of course, if someone spotted him he could always lie and say he was coming over to check on me.

I tossed the note down and stood up. It was too late to be thinking about any of this. I was exhausted. It had been a hell of a day. And right now I had to find a midnight snack for a demanding cat and hope and pray that I might fall back to sleep.

❁ ❁ ❁ ❁ ❁ ❁

The next morning, after waking up several times in the night, I forced myself not to look at the note on the coffee table. I washed with the same bucket of water and pulled on a pair of twill capris with a cotton eyelet top.

I was fast coming to the point where I was going to need to see about laundering my clothes. A depressing vision popped into my head of me pounding my clothes against a flat rock in the nearest river.

There was still a piece of *Tomme de Savoie* and a quickly aging pear in the fridge. I'd broken down and given Neige the last piece of tuna the night before. He thanked me of course by ignoring me the rest of the night except for the time when he swatted me in the face just when I was about to drop off.

By the time I finally awoke my sleepless night had pushed me into two mental camps. I either knew for sure that I was onto something about whoever had hurt Lilou and therefore needed to continue doing exactly what I was doing. *Or* I needed to quit immediately and possibly pen an *I'm sorry* note to tack to my front door so the killer would know that killing *me* would not be necessary.

I went to the balcony and glanced at where Lilou's body had been found. A couple of the weeds and tall grasses looked mashed down where the police had trampled the area but otherwise it just looked like an overgrown garden.

Not a place of terror where one mentally handicapped girl met her death.

I wiped sweat from my top lip.

I picked up the note. *Leave Lilou alone or you are nect.*

All of a sudden I was filled with anger. By the light of the day, I was seeing this note as less of a warning and more of an attack in its own right. And while on the one hand that made it seem more sinister, it also made it more galling.

I knew then that I couldn't go to Luc with it. And I couldn't stop what I was doing.

That's that then.

I may not be able to wash and fluff-dry my clothes or have another mojito in my lifetime, but by God I can find justice for this poor girl who never meant anyone any harm.

Feeling a hundred per cent better now that I knew the writer of that note hadn't cowed me, I mapped out my day, put ten euros in the Kate Spade shoulder bag that perfectly matched my shoes, and left the apartment.

I knocked on the old ladies' apartment door and Madame C opened it, her eyes bright. First thing she did was look at my empty hands so I knew the two of them were hungry. I mimed the act of eating and pointed to the stairs in an attempt to tell them I was going out for groceries.

The expression on her face told me she had no earthly idea of what I was saying. I glanced down the hall to see if there was any way Merci was available but Madame C shook her head.

"*Merci n'est pas ici*," she said.

I guessed she was telling me Merci wasn't home so I shrugged, kept my smile plastered across my face for her benefit and turned to go downstairs.

"I'll come back with take-out," I said in a joking voice, knowing she wouldn't understand my words.

Once outside, I looked up and down the cobblestone lane. It looked deserted but, to be fair, it had looked that way before the EMP went off too. These streets were so narrow it was a wonder vehicles ever made it down them.

The car that had stalled here three days ago had obviously been dragged away somehow because the lane was now clear. I was surprised anyone would bother. It wasn't like this street was a major thoroughfare or anything.

Not only did I not see cars but more importantly I did not see people. If anyone was watching me to see how I might be taking my midnight mail delivery, I wanted them to see without doubt that I was unaffected by their threats. I'm not sure why this was important to me. I'd been so focused on finding clues about Lilou's murder that I hadn't once looked over my shoulder to see if anyone was watching *me*.

My plan today was pretty basic. Step One: Let anyone who's watching me know I won't be swayed that easily. *Check*, I thought as I tugged my Chanel blue jean jacket into place over my capris. Would a woman cowering in fear over a death threat wear Chanel? I think not.

Step Two: Go to the market and load up as much as ten euros would buy me. Probably bread, cheese and whatever vegetables they had. And Step Three: Retrace Lilou's path that last day from the canal back to my apartment garden.

When I'd walked it yesterday, I'd been too miserable, cold and wet—and frankly despondent over the ruined corset—to look around. I'd remedy that today.

That's it. After that, I'd make dinner for the Madame Twins and hope to find either a cheap bottle of wine at the market, or that Guy, Luc or Jim would happen by with one.

❋❋❋❋❋❋

As I wove my way through the market, my basket bulging with every step, I could not imagine how any place in the world was handling the apocalypse better than the south of France.

Not only had Katrine been so thrilled about a new batch of *fromage de meaux* cheese that she insisted I take a sizable portion home with me, but there were effing truffles! I kid you not.

The world has come to an end, there are riots in the street in Detroit and Chicago but in the village of Chabanel we are eating shaved truffles on our omelets. But of course!

Not only that, but the village café I passed on the way to the market had every single table filled with people sipping coffees, chatting and reading paperbacks.

Was this a classic example of the ant and the grasshopper—with France the veritable grasshopper—or was the rest of the world dramatically over-reacting to one little blackout?

I passed Milleni's on the way back to the apartment and it had a line out the door and the aroma of sugar and vanilla wafting into the bright sunshine was very nearly transportive for all lucky passersby like me.

I'd picked up bread at the market, believing that almond croissants and *pain au chocolat* fell solidly under the category of *dancing while Lyons burned*, but I couldn't help but feel as I walked away from the *patisserie* full of glossy fruit tarts and breathtaking napoleons that the end of modern civilization probably ranked as the one time you really needed a dusting of sugar crystals.

As soon as I got back to the apartment, I ran upstairs and put away my groceries. Then I switched out my shoes to my Nancy Drew sleuthing slippers—which I named as I was slipping them on. They had thick athletic soles but they were low cut and did not need lacing.

Admittedly, they were prettier than they were practical—kind of my life's mantra—but they'd be more comfortable for the twenty-minute hike to the canal and back than the very stylish espadrilles I'd worn to the market.

This time on the way to the canal I was careful to be aware of my environment since as unpopulated as my neighborhood was, Chabanel was even sparser the further out I went. I wished I had a weapon of some kind since one thing I knew for sure was that the time-proven fall-back of the average woman—screaming your head off—would likely not be as effective these days.

In any case, I spent my time during the walk either trying to make sure I wasn't being followed or trying to see if there was anything along the road that might be a clue about Lilou's journey four days earlier. Unfortunately, I wasn't sure there weren't a couple of different ways to get to the canal and since I didn't know any but one I could only hope for the best.

Pretty crap detective procedure, I know. But there you are.

By the time I saw the canal I had talked myself into believing that *seeing* it was as far as I needed to go and promptly turned around.

It immediately started to rain. While glad I was wearing cheap canvas pull-on sneakers and equally glad that my denim jacket today wouldn't be destroyed by a gentle rainfall, I still wasn't delighted to return home yet again sopping wet.

I scanned the street on both sides for any sign of movement and then began to walk back to my neighborhood. I looked at every building and every window—most of them shuttered except for the very top ones—and examined every corner I came to.

Unlike in the States the streets in Chabanel have a single shallow wedged gutter in the middle of the lane where rain or refuse hosed from shop fronts travels down. Sewer grates punctuate the gutter every forty feet or so.

The streets looked ancient to me and I couldn't help but wonder if this was how they did things back in the twelfth century and instead of seeing what the rest of the world was doing in the way of improved gutters and sewers the villagers just couldn't be bothered to update.

Maybe it works for them, I thought as I continued to walk in the rain scanning the wrought iron Juliette balconies and blue shuttered windows, wondering who lived in these buildings.

The village church on Place des Martyrs was one street over from my street and for whatever reason known only to the sexton, its bells began to ring.

The sound of the bells was sonorous but melodic and they went on and on giving some kind of message to the villagers who obviously knew what the ringing meant.

On the one hand, it was rather comforting to hear them because it reminded me I was close to my apartment. But I couldn't help but wonder why they were ringing. It wasn't Sunday, and all I could think of was that line in the John Donne poem: "*No man is an island, entire of itself...any man's death diminishes me because I am involved in mankind, and therefore never send to know for whom the bell tolls. It tolls for thee.*"

So I know that might sound a little morbid but I have to say I actually felt better after remembering the words. Somehow it made me feel not so alone.

By the time I reached rue de Gaston de Saporta, not only was it raining harder, but the light was fading. I hadn't stopped to eat lunch and I was officially starving. I was startled to realize that the bulk of the day was slipping away.

Unless this lack of light was some kind of dark nuclear winter coming on?

It would have been great if I hadn't slept through science class in high school. I made a mental note to ask Guy or Jim about it. Admittedly, Thibault was probably a more likely candidate for knowing the answer but I resisted the thought of spending time with a guy who didn't seem to know about the invention of shampoo.

As soon as I reached the alley that I'd gone down two days earlier looking for the Madame Twins' cat Camille, I'd made up my mind that I was going to go ahead and search the garden, rain or not. The fact was I was already wet. What difference did it make?

Besides, the rain was probably quickly erasing any possible clues or evidence that the cops had missed—I was counting on them having missed something vital of course

—so the sooner I did my own sweep of the garden the better.

Jogging down the narrow alley, I hadn't taken into account the emotional backlash of my previous trip here. I put my hand out on the flat stonewall and felt my breathing start to speed up. Fortunately by the time I reached the entrance to the garden, I'd managed to catch my breath but already I was deciding that this was a bad idea.

Glancing up at the balcony of my apartment, I was relieved not to see any shadows or movement that might indicate someone had broken in and was lying in wait for me.

Always good.

I could see deep rutted tracks where the cops had brought the wagon across the garden. I could also see the hoof prints of the horse that had pulled the wagon. My stomach lurched as I ran the movie reel in my head of how they must have taken Lilou's body out. But I quickly forced myself to concentrate on examining the area for anything the cops might have missed.

At one point, near where I'd seen Lilou's arm, I got on my hands and knees to look around from that point of view.

You know how they always say you find a lost object in the very last place you look? Well, I do get the joke, trust me. But after twenty minutes of walking around the garden and stepping over snarling, scratching wild rose bushes and broken pieces of pottery I got to the point where I told myself I'd look at *one* last place—over nearer to my balcony—and then call it a day.

So of course that's when I found it.

Now, it is entirely possible that people throw junk back here although I hadn't found anything else like that, and it's also possible that the people whose apartments back up to this garden might toss things out the window from time to time although, again, that doesn't make a whole lot of sense.

But when I saw the strange glittering object under a layer of matted grass and weeds, my first thought was: *this doesn't belong here*. I reached for it and felt my heart pounding in my ears because I knew, *I just knew*, that this had to do with Lilou.

It was a metal disc about half the size of my palm with a hole in the center. It looked new, not like it had been here since Roman times or anything. And while it's true I had no idea of what the heck it was, it did occur to me that not only had Hugo gone into this garden the day Lilou was killed but his apartment was one of the ones that backed up to it.

I slid the odd disc into my pocket and turned to leave. When I did, my eye caught movement above me in one of the apartments. *Hugo's* apartment.

Hoping desperately that he didn't have a high-powered rifle set up on a tripod with my back in the crosshairs, I bolted from the garden, my heart racing as I held back a scream.

Once I hit the alley, I felt protected although I knew I had to then take the corner, go into my building and up the stairway—*where Hugo was*.

He's seen me out there, I thought. *He knows I found something.*

For a minute I wasn't completely sure I should even go home. If he was waiting for me, perhaps I should run to the police station and get Luc first?

And tell him what exactly? Tell him I found a metal disc and am now afraid to go home?

As I was trying to decide what I should do, I reached the end of the alley and saw a figure standing in the rain in the front of my apartment building.

I clutched the side of the stone wall before I saw that it wasn't Hugo but Merci. She was getting drenched and was looking up and down the street, all the while bouncing on the balls of her feet in agitation.

I emerged from the alley and immediately she turned to me.

"Oh, *merde*! Jules!" she said, her face white with dismay. "Come quick! Emergency!"

"What's happened?" I said as images of both the old ladies murdered in their armchairs ricocheted through my brain.

"Do you know CPO?" she said, tugging me toward the apartment door.

"Do you mean CPR?"

"Hurry! Before it's too late!"

Susan Kiernan-Lewis

18

Bad Moon Rising

Hugo sat in an armchair in front of a telescope pointed out the balcony. His head was slumped onto his chest as if he were examining his shirt buttons.

The cold hard fact was that he wouldn't be examining anything ever again.

I think I stood in Hugo's apartment and stared for at least twenty seconds before I even thought to shut my gaping mouth. Merci was wringing her hands and looking from Hugo to me but it should have been apparent even to her that no amount of correct letters in the alphabet was going to help Hugo now.

I walked over to him like I knew what I was doing and placed two fingers against where I knew his carotid artery was. Nothing. Not only that, he was cold.

The balcony door was open but it was not chilly by any stretch of the imagination. Hugo was cold because he'd been dead for several hours.

"How did you happen to find him?" I asked, careful not to touch any of his peeping tom equipment in case the cops were interested although I'm not sure why they would be now.

"He keeps his door unlocked," Merci said, "in case I need to borrow his Le Creuset casserole pan when he's out."

I looked at Merci. Was she really friends with this strange dude? Were our cultures really so different that the same guy I considered a budding serial killer or at the very least a mega sleezoid, was for Merci just someone she saw as an oddly quiet neighbor?

Or was Merci just sort of clueless?

"*Non*, Hugo!"

I turned to see both little old ladies standing in the doorway. Behind them a few more people from the apartment building had gathered.

"*Est-il mort?*" Madame C said stepping gingerly into the room.

Merci nodded sadly. "*Oui.*"

The two old ladies clucked and shook their heads.

"Do you have any idea how he died?" Merci asked, chewing on a nail and staring at the body.

I squatted by the chair and looked at his face as if that would tell me anything. I couldn't see any wounds at all.

"Maybe he just dropped dead?" I said. "Did he have a heart condition or anything that you know of?"

Madame B rattled off something to Merci who then looked at me and said, "She said he had a pacemaker. If he had a bad heart then why didn't the pacemaker work?"

I stood up. My clothes were still so wet I was already chafing.

"Maybe it got fried with the EMP," I said. "He should have gone to the hospital to get it sorted out before something like this happened." As much as I disliked Hugo this was starting to look like a truly senseless death. There was simply no need for it to have happened. I felt a flush of anger.

Plus, of course, there was the annoying fact that he'd been my prime suspect. If he *had* killed Lilou, there would certainly be no beating a confession out of him now.

"Jules?"

I turned to look at Merci who had a blanket in her hands.

"Should we cover him?"

I watched the Madame Twins over Merci's shoulder and felt an urgency grip me.

"Merci, please tell the sisters that if they've got any health issue like diabetes or chemo or *whatever* they need to let me or you know. The mayor said the Aix hospital is working and if Hugo had gone there, he'd still be alive."

Merci draped the blanket over the body and then turned and dutifully translated my words to the old ladies who alternately nodded and shrugged. A knock on the door revealed Guy in the doorway, his eyes wide and curious. He spoke to Merci and then left.

"Guy will get the priest," Merci said.

Great. So there's that sorted, I thought, beginning to edge my way out of the room.

A heavyset woman blocked my path, ending any debate about whether or not French women do or do not get fat. She snarled something at me, blasting me with a stench of garlic breath in the process.

"Whoa, Babette," I said, putting my hands up to ward her off. "Just passing through, *s'il vous plait*."

The lady began yelling to the people in the hallway and a few of them entered the room to get a look at both me and the dead body. From their expressions, I'm not sure which they were more repulsed by.

"*Excusez-moi*," I said, still trying to get past the obnoxious French woman when she began to shriek. I heard the word *Americaine* and something that sounded like *putain* which I knew wasn't good.

Either this cow thought I killed Hugo or she was blaming me for the fact that we were all standing here in an eleventh century building with no plumbing, lights or refrigeration.

"*Tais toi!*" Merci screamed at her. Then she said a bunch of other stuff and gestured to poor old Hugo which made the woman—after giving me one last glower—turn and leave the apartment.

"She's blaming me for the EMP, isn't she?" I said to Merci.

"It doesn't matter. She's just a crazy old hag who's always causing trouble."

That may be true but it didn't negate the fact that the old broad was saying exactly what everyone else here was thinking.

I was the American whose country probably did *something* to *someone* that made this happen to us. Likely the US bombed a country in the Middle East and they bombed our allies in retaliation. But however it happened, everyone agreed that America was probably at the center of it.

It looked like Merci had things under control now and I decided that my big red white and blue presence was probably not prudent especially when it intersected with calamity. I slipped out the door, my clothes squeaking and rubbing me in all the wrong places as I went.

I wasn't sure how Hugo's neighbors would handle his death beyond calling for the priest. There didn't seem any point in bothering the police with this. It didn't look like foul play. If there was any family, somebody would track them down. As for the burial, well, thank goodness that was on somebody else's to-do list.

Dying to get out of my wet clothes, I hurried down the hall to my apartment. I couldn't wait to have a moment to myself to try to sort out what I'd learned from my trek to the canal and back.

Plus, while it was still somewhat light out, I planned on making a *charcuterie* board with the pickles, olives, cheese and salami I'd picked up at the market. Once things calmed down a little bit in the building, I'd bring it over to the Madame twins. If Merci and Guy were around there should be enough for them too.

Satisfied that the rest of my evening was outlined the best it could be under the circumstances, I opened the door to my apartment.

I stepped through my door and froze.

My furniture was upside down. Pictures were torn from the wall and lay broken on the rug. And my clothes were scattered around the room and balcony.

19

A Whiter Shade of Hell

There's something nauseating about knowing a stranger has touched all your things.

And not just in the way that the TSA or airport security touches your stuff, but touched them in a way that feels riddled with hate and revulsion.

As I looked at my things—normally carefully folded and stacked—thrown on the floor and under the couch, I felt an indescribably strong urge to flee. When I choked down that response I forced myself to search the apartment.

Later, it would astound me that I didn't think that the burglar might still be in the apartment. Instead of backing away from the scene of the crime like a normal person, once I'd gotten a hold of myself the first thing I did was run to the kitchen to see if my food was still there. Amazingly, it was.

Whoever had done this either wasn't interested in robbing me or was too stupid to know that the things we now considered valuable had changed over night.

On the other hand, I soon discovered that my batteries were gone, along with my flashlight, all my money and every candle in the apartment.

Once I was sure I was alone, I set about trying to straighten the mess. My hands shook as I did it and even though I was still wet through from the rainfall earlier in the afternoon, it wasn't a physical chill that was making me shake.

Was this the same guy who'd written the note?

Was this an escalation of the threat?

Was this in answer to my boldly sashaying down the street this morning as if to say *you can't scare me*?

Because I have to say, I was scared.

Once I had the scattered clothes back in my suitcase—I guess I was still hopeful that I was going somewhere—I peeled off my wet clothes and used a towel to rub the blueness out of my thighs and arms. I pulled on dry yoga pants and a cashmere sweater and sat down on the couch and watched the last of the light leach from the sky.

I could hear noise and voices in the hallway as more and more people came to deal with the Hugo situation and yet I felt so totally alone and vulnerable.

I am a stranger in a strange land.

I have a roof over my head. But no money and no lights.

I have an enemy who wishes me harm.

And now I know that enemy could not have been Hugo. Not unless tossing my apartment was what brought on his heart attack.

So did this mean that Hugo *didn't* kill Lilou or was his dying irrelevant to that?

As I sat in my darkening living room, trying not to think how terrible my situation had now become, I forced myself to examine why I'd thought Hugo was the best candidate to be Lilou's murderer.

Finally after a frustrating and fruitless fifteen minutes, I had to admit that I had no reason for believing in his guilt beyond the fact that I thought he was a greasy perve.

It's one thing to go on instinct or listen to your gut but it's a totally different thing to make up your mind about someone based on things that have nothing to do with actual facts.

As I sat there in the dark, berating myself and feeling my life spiral out of control and down a long and very dark pit a thought struck me.

Is that what went wrong with me and Gilbert?

The fact was I hadn't thought about Gilbert for at least two days. And now, thinking I'd wronged him and that our not getting married was completely the result of my own actions, well, it was pretty much the cherry on my cake for one of the worst days of my life.

I was mere milliseconds from clapping my hands to my face for a royal boo-hoo—something which I'd be very sorry for later if I'd indulged as it happened—when there was a knock at my door. I sat and stared at the door.

It wouldn't be Merci. She was busy planning a funeral. The Madame Twins never bothered knocking.

"Jules?" Luc's voice came muffled but strong through the door.

Instantly I was on my feet and running to the door. I jerked it open and was never more happy to see anyone in my life. His smile dropped when he saw I'd been sitting in the dark.

"What's happened?" he said, coming in and glancing around the darkened room. "Where are your lights?"

He pulled out a flashlight and set down the paper bag that revealed a bottle of wine inside.

And so naturally I burst into tears.

※※※※※

Luc knew more about food and how to plate it up than any chef up and down Buckhead I'd ever seen. As I was pulling myself together he was laying out a feast on my coffee table: a bowl of green olives sprinkled with parsley and garlic, a small pot of olive oil next to the baguette I'd bought that day, the salami slices and of course the selections of cheeses that Katrine had given me.

"How did you know to come?" I asked, feeling much better after my second glass of the very lovely rosé he had brought. For the second night in a row he'd come at just the right time.

"Just doing my rounds and I ran into Guy Joslin. He told me what happened."

"Will you investigate it?"

"Seems very straightforward but my sergeant will take a statement from everyone present."

I nodded. His answer still didn't explain how he happened to have a bottle of rosé in his hand at the time he was doing his rounds but I was willing to believe that walking around with a bottle of wine was probably standard operating procedure for most Frenchmen.

"You walk a beat?" I asked.

"Only certain neighborhoods."

"Because of the murder."

"Bien sûr."

I knew he wasn't totally telling the truth. He walked the beat because Lilou was an unsolved murder, true. But he walked the beat that included my apartment and knocked on my door two nights in a row because of me.

Was it because I was American? Had he gotten info from the Consulate in Aix about treating the stranded American nationals with kid gloves?

"You are positive you locked the door when you left this morning?" he asked.

"Of course, Luc," I said with mild exasperation. "I'm from Atlanta. I don't walk to my mailbox without locking my door."

He smiled grimly. I saw that a few of my silky underthings were still scattered across the floor where I hadn't gotten to them yet.

"I thought that maybe Hugo might have been the one who killed Lilou," I said.

"Why is that?"

"Because he's shifty and he had opportunity. Plus I met him immediately after I discovered the body."

Luc frowned. "Did you tell me that in your statement?"

"I'm not sure I gave a full statement. We were interrupted by the EMP. But in any case Hugo couldn't be the one who broke into my apartment. He'd been dead for hours. Probably most of the day."

"Why would Hugo want to trash your apartment?"

I went to the kitchen and found the note in one of the drawers and brought it back to him.

"This was shoved under my door two nights ago," I said. "I think it's reasonable to think it was written by the murderer, don't you?"

Luc stared at the note with his mouth open.

"You got this the night before last?" he asked.

"Yes, and before you get all mad about why I didn't come to you, I know how busy you are."

"This is a threat, Jules," he said evenly.

"Trust me, I was adequately freaked out when I got it."

He set the note down next to the *fromage de meaux* on the coffee table.

"And what have you been doing to make the writer of this note feel you are getting too close?"

"Aside from being tossed in the canal? Do you believe me *now* that I didn't slip?"

"I think you are playing a dangerous game and you need to stop immediately," he said sternly.

I have to admit, even though the light wasn't all that good with just his single flashlight Luc still looked incredibly sexy getting all protective and alpha male with me right about then. It gave me very nice butterflies in my tummy.

As long as he didn't try to stop me from continuing my investigation.

I quickly filled him in on what I'd done by talking to the parents and retracing Lilou's steps the day she was killed. He listened quietly and didn't once shake his finger at me or try to ground me or anything.

"So you interviewed her parents," Luc said, "traced Lilou's steps from the canal to where her body was found and...anything else?"

This would be the part where I tell him about Jim. I mean, if this was any typical made-for-TV thriller this is exactly the place where I would come clean about what Lilou's mother said, and if I *don't* come clean, then it would also be the reason—as anybody who's ever watched a television drama knows—why I will eventually pay the price for that omission by having my throat slit by the very guy I'm trying to protect.

"Nope," I said. "I did find a weird gee-gaw thingy in the garden this afternoon that may have belonged to either Lilou or her killer." I jumped up again to extricate the flat metal disc that I'd stuck in the pocket of my wet capris.

I brought it to Luc and he used the flashlight to examine it thoroughly.

"Any idea what it is?" I asked.

"It's a part," he said. "Either to a machine or a mechanical device of some kind. It's not something on its own."

"You mean like a washer or something?"

"Basically."

"Could it be evidence?"

"I'm sorry, Jules," he said with the most condescending smile I have ever seen in my life. "It's just junk."

"No worries," I said with a shrug, determined that he wouldn't see my embarrassment.

The voices in the hallway stayed at a steady hum so I could only assume that more people had come to pay their respects or whatever one does with an unexpected body on a Wednesday evening.

I actually smelled meat grilling so it seemed the Madame Twins would have their dinner tonight after all what with all the people bringing food in an apocalyptic version of a French wake.

Luc and I listened silently for awhile. I was very conscious of him sitting next to me. Very conscious of all the millions of things he probably should be doing tonight instead of sitting with me.

It was pretty clear he liked me. And when facing the end of the world there are worse things than having the guy with all the guns like you.

"They stole my money," I said as I smeared the last of the tapenade on a piece of bread. "I'm not sure what I'm going to do with no money."

"Well, that was going to be the case very soon in any case," he said reasonably. "I'll have another lantern dropped by tomorrow as well as a spare flashlight."

"Thanks, Luc. I appreciate it." I looked around the room, illuminated only by the flashlight he'd laid on the table. I was pretty sure he'd leave it with me when he left.

"Why are you so determined to find out who hurt Lilou? You did not know her."

I thought about this for a moment although I could've answered him straightaway.

"It's because I know she's being swept under the rug," I said. "No offense. But you have your hands full. And asking questions and solving puzzles is kind of my thing. You ever heard of the expression *like a dog with a bone*?"

He nodded. "We have something similar in French."

"Well, that's who I am. There aren't a whole lot of times in life when being tenacious is a good thing. I know that for a fact. It's why I wanted to be an investigative journalist in the first place. Journalism is one of the few jobs where you can dig for answers and the more you dig, the closer you get to the truth."

"Did you always want to be a reporter?"

"Pretty much. I was planning on being a lawyer at one point because my father wanted me to. When he died, I guess I thought I was honoring him by going to law school."

"What happened?"

"I came to my senses before I ended up in horrendous student debt with a degree I didn't really want."

"What about your father?"

"I told myself I would honor him in other ways and whether or not I became a lawyer—well, he's dead so he wouldn't be affected by that one way or the other. What about you? Always want to be a cop?"

He laughed. "I suppose so, yes. But for me it's not so much about puzzles but right and wrong."

"Uh oh. I think I know which kid *you* were in school."

"*Exactement*," he said wagging his finger at me, but grinning. "And you should remember that, yes?"

❊❊❊❊❊❊

Jim paused at the arched entrance to the village cemetery and then moved quickly to the fringe of surrounding trees, careful not to trample the flowers that mourners had placed on the graves.

He was sure this was where they would lay Lilou. He imagined himself coming and putting flowers by her gravesite if they did.

Unless that would look too weird? The French were strange. If they saw him honoring Lilou, they might get ideas. It was bad enough he couldn't come to the funeral—if there was one. But the cops might be watching. They did that sort of thing pre-EMP. Well, at least on *Law and Order* they did.

He felt flooded with guilt and sadness as he scanned the paltry cemetery. It was nestled just behind the church and yet there wasn't a soul here. Or at least not any walking around on two feet. He'd been right to come at dusk.

He couldn't believe the cops hadn't talked to him yet. Thank God for the EMP. They were too busy nowadays to ask the right questions. For Lilou's sake, he was sorry about that. For his own, well, he always was selfish.

Jules Hooker's face drifted into his mind and he felt himself flinching at the lie he'd told her. Could she tell? There had been something in her face when he said it that made him think she could. Surely he was imagining that?

On the other hand he'd been told in the past that he was a bad liar. The truth was always right there on his face for the world to see.

Just my luck.

As he turned to make his way out of the cemetery, his eyes fell on a bunch of plastic flowers and he told himself again that he would come back and put flowers by her headstone.

Could her parents afford such an extravagance?

He allowed himself a moment's fantasy to think that he would buy the headstone for Lilou. But he knew he wouldn't.

He couldn't.

Not without tipping off half the village.

20

Dots Connecting

It's hard to imagine waking up smiling the morning after your apartment was broken into, your neighbor died two doors down and you stand no chance of having a hot cup of coffee. But I did exactly that the next morning. Wake up smiling I mean.

Luc had stayed late the night before but before I could confess some of my more embarrassing moments during freshman year at the University of Florida he took his leave and yes, he left me his flashlight even though I was going straight to bed and didn't really need it and he definitely needed it to wander through the moonless streets of Chabanel after dark.

That no doubt contributed to my smile that morning. I liked Luc DeBray and he clearly liked me. I was not sure of the timing of beginning a romantic episode in any country other than my own—and obviously not there either—so I thought it was pretty safe to leave that to him.

Besides, I had the whole trying-to-stay-alive thing going on and that took up much of my time.

Right after I dressed and moments before I successfully polished off the remnants of last night's olives and *fromage de meaux* for breakfast, Luc's police lieutenant was pounding on my door.

He was a very sour-faced dude who'd obviously enjoyed a few too many beignets in his thirty-five years and who just as obviously hated being used as a delivery boy this morning.

Wordlessly—which considering the language thing was just as well—he handed me a lantern, a jug of kerosene and another flashlight, then turned on his heel and left. I felt a brief flash of guilt wondering if someone else needed these things more than I did but I have to say I didn't hesitate to accept them.

As I tucked the lantern and jug away in the cabinet under the sink—like a burglar wouldn't look there first—I allowed myself to wonder for the thousandth time about who broke in the night before.

While Luc and I had talked it to death last night, I still hadn't come up with a face for who might have done it. The lock hadn't been broken. Either someone had a key or scaled the wall outside to enter through the balcony or I'd forgotten to lock the door. Luc felt strongly that the break in was random and not someone I knew.

I wished I could believe that.

I quickly put the *pain au chocolat* and the remaining cheese into the bag that Luc had left last night and slipped out into the hallway. The rest of the apartment building was quiet. I went straight to the Madame Twins' apartment and lightly tapped on the door.

Madame B answered and immediately looked at the bag in my hands.

She rattled off a string of French and pointed to Hugo's apartment. I wasn't sure what she was saying. I shrugged apologetically.

"I'm going out," I said. "Are you okay?"

She nodded but didn't smile, her eyes still on the bag in my hands. "Okay," she said.

"Here's some cheese and day-old bread." I handed her the bag which she opened. A flicker of a smile graced her lips.

Yay. Score one for Team USA.

I hurried down the stairs and out the front door. Once on the street I was astonished at how beautiful the weather was this morning. There was a light breeze but it was already warm and the sun was filtering through the big leaves of the plane trees along the road, giving a dappling effect that—are you ready for this?— made me happy to be alive.

Boy, a few more mornings like this and I really will start my day singing.

Cue the villagers with the tar and pitchforks.

As I walked into the center of the village I resolved to hit the market for whatever I could find for tonight's dinner using the ten euros that Luc left me on the coffee table before he left last night—another reason why I was glad nothing happened between us.

Just thinking of being officially broke instead of wondering at what time in the future that would happen made me double down on the problem of how I was going to make a living in a foreign village.

Should I move to Aix? It was a bigger city and there were a lot more Americans there. Plus there was the American consulate. Granted, Luc said there were more problems in Aix too. And the consulate had been closed since the EMP went off.

And honestly I'm not sure how much help it would be to have a bunch of Americans around. I was never much of a joiner. And since they're in the same spot I am we'd probably all be vying for the same English-speaking work. Probably wiser to just stay put.

But stay put and do what? It's all very well for Guy or Thibault to create hand crank walkie-talkies or water purification devices but nobody was going to give *me* a corn dog for anything I could do.

I briefly thought of Katrine the cheese lady and decided I'd ask her if she needed help stacking her cheese wheels or something. If she paid me in cheese I'd no doubt die from a colon blockage before the year was out but it might beat starving.

I hadn't forgotten Jim Anderson's suggestion that I work with him on the Chabanel newspaper. But first I couldn't imagine there was enough work for the both of us and secondly there was that whole *maybe-he's-a-murderer* thing.

I paused on the corner before plunging across the main village street to the market in order to allow myself a moment of reflection.

Did I have a gut reaction to my suspicions about Jim? And if I did, should I trust it?

I tried to pay attention to how I felt about the possibility that Jim had killed Lilou and I have to admit it felt bad.

If what Lilou's mother said was true then Jim flat out lied to me about knowing Lilou. So do I believe my countryman or an ex-prostitute grieving mother with an axe to grind? Is it possible she was just mistaken?

That didn't fly at all. A six-foot four American in a small French village? There was nobody in the village who didn't know him.

No. Lilou's mother hadn't made a mistake.

As I crossed the street, I realized I needed to talk to Jim. Face to face and straight up ask him: *Why did you lie about knowing Lilou?*

Yeah, that ought to put him at ease, I thought with a tremor of unease. *Be sure you find a nice dark alley to ask him in.*

In any case I had no idea how to find Jim. I could have asked Luc last night but then I would have tipped my hand.

I didn't want Luc thinking I was interested in Jim as a possible suspect.

Perhaps if I went back to the café near the *boulangerie* where I saw Jim last? Where he gave me the tip that ended up by my being assaulted and tossed in the canal?

I shook that negative thought out of my head. No preconceived theories, I told myself sternly. *Innocent until proven guilty*.

Satisfied that this was a good way to check Jim off my suspects list once and for all, I strode to Katrine's booth. Today it was tucked away between the fishmonger and the poultry guy and I could see she was doing a brisk business.

Forget that the world is ending, I thought with amazement as I got in line, *the French need their cheese*! Katrine and her husband must be pretty confident about making a living no matter the world order since, let's face it, as long as you have goats or cows, you've got product. And in France you've got customers willing to wait in line for it before water, shelter or life-saving insulin. Just saying.

I watched Katrine interact with her customers— smiling, laughing and wrapping up wedges, slices and wheels of every imaginable kind of cheese. A heavyset man stood next to her. He wore an apron and was weighing, cutting and wrapping chunks and wheels of cheese as intensely as Katrine. I assumed this must be her husband Gaultier.

Katrine spotted me as I edged closer and turned and spoke quickly to her husband. By the time I reached the front of the line, she had already wrapped a package of cheese for me and was pulling off her apron.

"*Bonjour*, Jules!" she said cheerfully, leaning over to kiss me on both cheeks.

"Wow, you guys are doing a good business," I said, shaking my head in amazement.

She surprised me by taking my arm and pulling me away from the stand.

"I am having a break, yes?" she said as she tucked the cheese package into my string bag and slid her arm through mine.

❊❊❊❊❊❊

Katrine quickly led me away from her cheese booth and I have to say it didn't feel so much like I was about to have coffee with a girlfriend as it did like I was being kidnapped.

But Katrine had given me a whole lot of free cheese in the last three days and was one of the few people in the village who actually smiled at me so I was willing to give her the benefit of the doubt.

We moved down a narrow side street that—like so many of the streets of Chabanel—at first glance looked deserted. Inside a slight recess hidden by a jutting of crumbling stone wall was a tiny bistro table with two chairs set in front of a quaint café. Katrine waved to someone through the café window and settled down in one of the chairs. She instantly lit up a cigarette and offered me one.

I shook my head.

Now that I had a moment to see Katrine without the constant movement I'd always seen her before, I could see that her face was clenched with stress.

"You okay, Katrine?" I asked.

"*Bien sûr!*" she said with forced jolliness. "Why are you asking?" But she looked away as if she wasn't really interested in hearing my reasons.

I know a lot of people are private and closed—even if I'm not. And as a would-be investigative reporter, I know that not everybody wants to spill their most intimate details. But the French take that whole *holding their cards close* thing even further than most people.

As the waiter set down two espressos I realized that Katrine had befriended me very quickly and right at this moment I was beginning to wonder why.

"Have you been in Chabanel all your life?" I asked.

She drew on her cigarette and smiled. "Of course. Most people here have."

"So you know everyone in town pretty much?"

Her eyes narrowed. Honestly, it was the first semi-unfriendly thing she'd done since I'd met her.

"*Bien sûr*," she said.

"Wow. That's great," I said cheerfully. "I could use a quick run down of who's who in Chabanel."

She frowned in confusion.

"Like Madame Cazaly and Madame Becque?" I asked. "Do you know them?"

Katrine seemed to relax for a moment.

"The twins? Everyone knows them. Do you not know their story?"

"No, but I'd love to."

She stubbed out her cigarette and drank her coffee in one swig.

"Those two are a village legend. One married, one did not. When the married one became widowed, they moved in together. But they were always close."

So far I'd guessed this much.

"So, what makes them a legend?" I pressed.

Katrine lit up another cigarette. Her face softened and she looked beyond me as if envisioning the sisters a long time ago.

"They were in *La Résistance* during the war."

"Really?" I felt my pulse escalate. "That's pretty gutsy."

"*Mais, oui*," Katrine said with a sad smile. "The sisters are always being very gutsy."

The way she said that gave me the feeling that something awful had happened to the sisters during that time. I know a lot of bad things happened during the war. But Katrine's reluctance to tell me specifics sixty years later made me think there was a very sad story here.

"I must get back," she said, standing up.

I opened my purse but she waved her hand.

"It is being on the house," she said. "The owner is a friend of mine."

"That's...well, thanks, Katrine. Every time I turn around, you're being so nice to me."

I didn't mean to say that. As soon as I did I knew it came out sounding suspicious. But the truth was as grateful as I was for her friendship a part of me wasn't sure why she'd picked me to embrace out of everyone who wandered up to her booth.

I know that's terribly ungenerous of me and I felt instantly bad that I'd probably insulted her. She deserved better than my cynicism.

Still standing, Katrine turned to look at me, her smile firmly in place but looking a whole lot less genuine now.

"It is what friends do, *n'est-ce pas?*" she said ominously.

21

One Step Over the Line

Luc's stomach was growling by the time Mayor Beaufait called him into her office. If he thought the police station was crowded with problems and people attached to them, the mayor's office was much worse. The difference was that Lola Beaufait seemed to thrive on it.

"Well, well, Luc," she said cheerfully, gesturing for him to take a seat in the bone white Versailles settee opposite her ornate Louis XIV style desk. Her entire office was designed in the so-called golden age of French decorative style.

Luc would have thought that might send the wrong message but Madame Beaufait had been mayor at Chabanel for over a decade so obviously not.

"How are we doing in Chabanel today?" she said as she crossed her legs and worked a high-heeled Christian Louboutin pump off one foot and dropped it on the floor with a wince.

"Not bad," Luc said truthfully. "We are still waiting for some supplies from Aix. Petrol. Vehicles."

"Are all the cafés running?"

"More or less. The *boulangeries* are running short of supplies."

Beaufait nodded and wrote something down on a pad.

"Crime?" she asked, still writing.

"Not more than usual."

"Excellent. I'm having some of my people going around to check on the old ones to make sure they have what they need."

Luc didn't dislike Lola Beaufait. After so long in office people liked her and respected her. Although she might easily trample a few toes in the process she'd get the job done.

But he knew her "people" weren't helping "the old ones" so much as they were going to their neighbors and encouraging them to step forward. Luc didn't fault Beaufait for that. He knew her office couldn't support everyone in the village who needed help.

It was right that people should be encouraged to step forward to help the weaker ones in the village.

"Any news from Aix?" Luc asked. "Or Paris?"

"Regarding what?" She waved a hand around her office. It was illuminated by two silver-plated oil lanterns that gave off a fragrant wafting of lavender and beeswax. "*This* is the new normal, Luc. The sooner *we* get used to it at the top level, the sooner we'll help the rest of Chabanel to accept it."

"I meant, any news on who caused it."

"Does it matter? Iraq or possibly Russia." She shrugged and Luc had to admit it all added up to the same thing.

"What about your homicide?" Lola asked with a frown. "Can you wrap that up?"

"You know we no longer have access to any lab facilities. And there were no witnesses."

"The autopsy?"

Luc flinched at the mayor's coldness but tried to push it away. Lola didn't know Lilou. Of course she wouldn't.

"She was strangled. No sexual congress," he said.

"But a man did it?"

"Almost certainly."

"Close the case."

Luc knew his mouth fell open. The mayor had never interfered with his office before. It didn't bode well going forward.

"I can't close it until I solve it," he said slowly.

"Then make it a cold case and set it aside. Indefinitely."

"May I ask why?"

The mayor looked around her office in a pantomime of astonishment and frustration.

"You have to ask? I don't care how much we try to make it look normal, Luc, this is no longer business as usual! Lilou Basso was the damaged daughter of the village whore and the town drunk. You will not waste any more time or resources trying to figure out who killed her."

"Mentally challenged."

"Excuse me?"

"Lilou wasn't damaged. She was mentally challenged."

"And you are coming dangerously close to insubordination, Luc." Lola narrowed her eyes at him. "I don't need you judging me. Are we clear?"

Luc nodded. The fact was, for just a moment it felt like he was acting toward Lola the way Matteo acted toward him. Even if Lola was morally wrong, it was idiotic to attempt to censor her.

"Sorry," he said, and meant it.

"Is that it?" She looked at her watch and then motioned through the glass door to her secretary to send in the next person.

"Just one more thing," Luc said. "We have an American tourist stranded in Chabanel. I was wondering if there was any way the village or your office could employ her. She has no money."

"Employ her? To do what?" Beaufait said, her expression incredulous.

"I don't know but otherwise how will she live?"

"That at least is one problem that will not land on my desk," Beaufait said firmly. "Take her to Aix. There's an American consulate there. She's their problem. Are we clear?"

Luc stood up. It wasn't the answer he wanted but it was pretty close to the one he'd expected.

※※※※※

After Katrine hurried back to her cheese booth, I couldn't help but think that whole *it's what friends do* thing meant she had set her sights on a favor she wanted from *me*.

I know that sounds terrible and maybe it's the reason I don't have that many friends but come on! You meet a total stranger—someone who is always giving you free stuff and kissing you and then when you ask *why* they make a comment that sounds like they expect reciprocity?

What would *you* think?

It was beyond me to imagine what Katrine thought I could possibly do for her except maybe help her with her conversational English language skills—something I couldn't imagine would any longer be a benefit.

But like most things that were a mystery to me, I knew obsessing over it wouldn't get me any closer to the truth.

But at least I had a nice wheel of cheese to share with the old ladies.

Just thinking of those two dressed in 1940's camo with rifles in their hands, hiding in the forests around Chabanel in order to strike at the Nazis had me shaking me head in amazement.

It was a difficult picture to put together. Especially Madame C and her constant look of uncertainty and fear.

I'd been right about them having already experienced a time in history when things were hard. At least nowadays people weren't actively trying to kill us.

Hopefully.

The café nearest the *boulangerie* where I last saw Jim was a couple streets away so I decided to chill there for the rest of the morning to see if he didn't walk past. It wasn't much of a plan but it was all I had. Besides, the weather was just so gorgeous.

It was after ten in the morning when I settled at one of the tables at the Café Sucre. There were only five tables and only two with umbrellas. There were more inside but nobody ever went inside. The outdoor café tables spilled out into the street.

There'd been no concern about cars before the EMP and there certainly were none now. As I sat there, enjoying the sun on my back, I thought, *you literally would not know from this spot that the rest of the world was struggling without infrastructure.*

Here people were laughing, drinking coffee, writing in journals and watching everyone else walk past.

Just as if nothing had happened!

I used one of Luc's euros to buy a *café crème*. I reasoned that if I got information that lead to Lilou's killer as a result of my time at the café, it would be well worth the price. I tipped my face to the sun and enjoyed the warmth. Plane trees bordered the square in front of the café and provided a canopy of dappled shade on the cobblestones. It was perfection.

An hour passed of sipping and sunning and during that time quite a few people gave me unfriendly looks as if they knew I was a foreigner, or worse—American. I'd read in a magazine on the flight over that the French don't respond to smiles the way Americans do. I think the article said the French believe that when you smile so much for no obvious reason, instead of thinking you're a friendly sort the French think you're up to something.

So I didn't smile back at the stares but I did order a *kir* with a small dish of olives. Hey, it was nearly lunchtime and I was working!

Moments after the waiter deposited my drink and olives on the table before me, I saw someone I recognized. I flinched at the sight and hoped he wouldn't see me but it was too late. We made eye contact and within seconds Thibault came over to my table.

"You look so French sitting here!" he said with a grin, his greasy hair slicked down across his forehead.

I must have gripped the café table with both hands and physically shuddered because he didn't make a move to kiss me. *Thank God.*

When I didn't respond, he said, "Hello! Do you remember me?"

"Yes, of course," I said, managing a smile and then losing it as soon as he pulled up a chair and sat down.

Next he signaled the waiter and then focused on my breasts as if he was looking for something there.

"Any more news from the US?" I asked tightly holding my wine glass in front of my chest to block his view the best I could.

"You are welcome to come to my apartment any time if you want to see what they're doing in Atlanta," he said with a wolfish grin.

"Thanks. I appreciate the offer," I said pleasantly. "I'll definitely keep it in mind."

Right after I stab a fork in my eye and put on extra sweaters because hell will have frozen over.

"It seems they are no worse off than we are but less able to handle the inconveniences." He shrugged.

As much as I didn't like to hear him criticize how the US was handling everything I had to admit he was probably right. It wasn't possible to believe that anybody in Cleveland was sitting at a café at noon sipping wine and watching the world go by. It was more likely that they were breaking windows and ransacking their local Jiffy Mart with the smell of burning tires lilting over the horizon.

"You look very French sitting here at the café," Thibault said again as the waiter brought him his *petit café*.

For me that was when the penny dropped. Those words, uttered by arguably the greasiest, most unkempt man in the village, made me realize the one thing I'd been missing up to now.

This whole new world order was about adapting. That was the only way anyone was going to survive. The people who made computer components yesterday were going to have to learn to milk cows or weave baskets today. The car mechanics were going to have to become experts in livestock management.

Entitled, sheltered American women were going to have to take several pages from the French playbook about how to live in a drastically changed world—something I had been resisting ever since I arrived in France. And that was even *before* the lights went out.

And while I'm sure I didn't look at all French in my Raybans and cropped pants, Thibault's comment made me realize that it was my resistance to acclimating to my new situation that was my major stumbling block so far. Even to the point that I'd recoiled at the thought of having Thibault join me for a drink.

And why? Because he's a greaser and a letch?

Yes. But even more than that was the fact that he's a human being who is in this mess with me. Even after the very limited time I'd spent with him I was pretty sure he wasn't evil or intending to hurt me. On the contrary, he knew how to contact my country and get information for me.

But even more than that, Thibault is a part of this village. *My* village now. That means he's a part of my life now.

True, he stares at my boobs but he probably doesn't even know he's doing it.

As soon as my mental landscape shifted at his words, so did my mood, my attitude and my view of my new life. I have to say a lot of things suddenly felt right. Like a piece of a puzzle that had been askew just clunked into place.

I eased back into my chair and felt the sun on my face and arms. It literally might have been the first time I'd relaxed since I arrived.

"So what are you doing this beautiful day?" I asked.

"I was supposed to see Guy today but I went fishing instead. So I am off to Aix to sell the fish at the market there."

"Aix is a long walk from Chabanel," I observed.

"I have a car."

My eyes widened. "I thought none of the cars were working now."

"It is true. Most cars built after 1988 no longer function. My CV2, however..." He shrugged and gave me a gap-toothed smile. "As long as the petrol holds out, I'm good."

Whoa. A friend with a ham radio and a car?

"Have you been to the village market yet this morning?" he asked.

"Briefly. But I need to go back. Why?"

He pulled a note from his shirt pocket and waved it.

"I have been tasked by Merci to pick up a kilo of *courgettes* and a few other things for Sunday lunch but I don't have time now."

I held out my hand for the grocery list. After all, you never knew when you'd need a return favor. *Did I mention the dude had a car?*

"Sure. I'll do it," I said. "Can I just take the groceries to Merci's?"

"*Oui*. Her mother Madame Joslin has a credit at the market. Just show the vendors her note."

The grocery list read, *2 kilos courgettes, 1 kilo chevre. Tomates, paté, du vin. Merci Joslin.*

"I guess this is how we'll be communicating for the foreseeable future," I said. "Passing notes in the twenty-second century."

"Probably," Thibault said as he dug a few coins out of his pocket, tossed them on the table and stood up. "*Merci, Jules. À bientôt.*"

And when he leaned over to kiss me on the cheek, I have to tell you suddenly it felt like the most natural thing in the world.

I watched him disappear down the street, and then turned to notice that he'd put enough money on the table for both our drinks and I felt a warm flush and reminded myself about not judging a book by its dust jacket when my eyes landed on the coins on the table and I swear I felt the tips of my fingers turn cold.

Almost knocking over my now empty *kir* glass, I reached for the coins and spread them out on the table. Two one-euro coins. A ten-penny coin.

And a small flat disk with a hole in it exactly like the one I'd found in the back garden.

I'm sure I must have stared at the coins for a full five minutes trying to figure out what it meant. Obviously Thibault had just emptied his pockets without thinking. He hadn't intended to throw down a useless washer among the coins.

But he had.

The longer I stared at that washer the more I knew it was connected to what had happened to Lilou. It took me that long for all the thoughts in my head to line up and begin to make sense and when they did, I literally gasped and jammed my hand into my string basket where I'd dropped Merci's grocery list on top of my package of cheese.

I placed it on the table before me and gently straightened out the page and re-read the words. Then, with trembling fingers, I dug into my pants pocket and drew out the note that had been shoved under my door. And lay the two notes side by side.

There could be no mistake. Not only was it the same handwriting. It was written on the same kind of paper as if ripped from the same notebook.

For a moment I just stared at the washer and then the two notes as if I didn't know what they signified. But my instinct was moving faster than my brain because I started to get angry before I even knew why.

And when my brain finally caught up with my burgeoning fury I realized it was because I now knew who killed Lilou Basso.

22

The Penny Drops

The boy's foot was stuck in the grate at the bottom of the ancient sewer. His friends—none of them older than ten—stood around and alternately giggled or harangued him.

Luc put his hand on the child's shoulder and tried to see how he could possibly have wiggled into the contraption. The mayor's office had suspended school for the remainder of the week even though Luc had asked for Chabanel to go on as normally as possible.

Children—especially little boys—with too much time on their hands and no TV or electronic games to fill it was a bad equation. The Madame Mayor's children were long grown and gone. Perhaps she had forgotten what little boys were like?

"*Maman* will kill me!" the trapped boy yelped frantically pawing at his leg in an attempt to free it.

"Just take his shoe off!" one boy yelled out.

The first thing Luc had noticed was that the boy's shoe was gone, obviously dropped to the bottom of the sewer. It wasn't the shoe that was the problem but the boy's foot. That's what was stuck.

Luc was going to have to remove the rust-encrusted bolts to lift the grate and from the looks of it they hadn't been turned since the grate had been set—possibly a hundred years earlier.

Luc instructed the other boys to stand back. He'd already tried to send them home and wouldn't waste his breath asking again. He sorely wished he had a cellphone to send for a toolbox back at the station. He stood at the lip of the sewer, gauging how filthy he was going to have to get when he caught movement in the street and glimpsed Jules Hooker crossing the street several blocks away heading toward her apartment.

She was moving quickly, purposefully. But then she was American. *That's how they all move until they start to gain the weight.* At least *that* was something Jules would no longer have to worry about. She would live in Chabanel and keep her slim figure, walking the village streets, climbing the many staircases, and keeping her arms toned by carrying her groceries. Luc felt a tingle of excitement picturing her figure in his mind.

"I need to pee!" the trapped boy yelled, setting off waves of laughter among his friends.

"You might have thought of that before you climbed down there," Luc said, resigning himself to a lengthy and very dirty end to his afternoon.

As the other boys began to cheer, Luc slowly lowered himself down to where the hapless—and shoeless—lad waited.

❊❊❊❊❊

A part of me thought about going to the *police municipale* first to see if Luc was available but as excited as I was I also had a very clear memory of that condescending look he'd given me over the metal washer I'd found.

The metal washer which now made perfect sense.

I saw the spires of the Église Saint-Sebastian church that heralded the start of the street my apartment was on and my excitement built even further. I was breathless with a sudden adrenaline rush at what I now knew and what was literally right around the corner.

Because I was so focused on where I was going and what I would do when I got there, I slammed right into someone on a bike as they came around the corner.

I went flying and felt two inches of elbow skin being left behind on the centuries old cobblestones as I hit the road. The pain jolted up my arms and both legs as I looked up from the tangle of bike chain and bouncing cheese wheels to see Katrine Pelletier sitting on the ground in front of me.

"What the hell, Katrine?" I said, although the collision was totally my fault. I pulled myself to my feet, checking to make sure nothing important was broken. I looked down the road as if expecting the apartment building to disappear before I could get there.

I glanced back at Katrine who was nursing a bloody knee and felt a shimmer of guilt for having caused the accident.

"Are you okay?" I asked somewhat begrudgingly.

I had to get home!

"I wanted to talk with you," Katrine said, looking unhappily at her bent bicycle. The front wheel continued to spin but it was no longer connected to anything that would produce propulsion.

"I thought we did that over coffee earlier," I said, holding a hand out to her. "Nice chat by the way."

I pulled her to her feet.

"I wanted to say I'm sorry."

"Can this wait?" I said as I turned away, deciding for the both of us that it could.

"Jules, no!" Katrine plucked at her skirt to keep it away from her bloody kneecap. "Please let me explain."

What is it with us women? I'm sure if I was Tom Cruise needing to defuse a ticking bomb in Time Square I would not waste any more time on girly she-said-she-said silliness. I knew that anything that needed to be straightened out between me and Katrine would be straightened out eventually but it didn't need to be *now*.

Except, could I really bash into her bike, bloody her knee and then run off and not listen to her apology? Good for Tom Cruise but I just couldn't do it.

"Can you make it fast?" As I heard the words come out of my mouth I realized that their harshness was probably worse than just running off but to her credit, Katrine didn't flinch. She left her bike in the road—what was there to fear? that a car might run over it?—and hobbled after me as I scooped up my bag and turned to continue my speed-walk toward my apartment.

"You have every right to wonder why I have artificially befriended you," she said breathlessly. "I'm sorry if I believed you too stupid to see through that."

Well, honestly, she'd been right. I *had* been too stupid or at least too self-absorbed to wonder why she was giving me free cheese, at least at first. But if this was her idea of an apology it was obvious we had a lot more differences than I'd imagined.

"The fact is you strongly resemble someone I know," Katrine said. "From the minute I saw you I knew there was going to be trouble."

Regardless of the fact that I was in a hurry to confront a killer, even I had to stop at that.

I turned to face Katrine. "For the love of God, what are you talking about?"

"My husband Gaultier," Katrine said, her face blushing furiously. "You look just like Zelie, his ex-wife."

"So?"

"He is still in love with her! *C'est tout.* I knew once he saw you..."

"Are you kidding me?"

I'm not saying Gaultier was a troll or anything, honestly, he wasn't that bad, but I couldn't imagine on what planet I'd be attracted to him. This Zelie must have two brain cells chasing around upstairs. And frankly I wasn't too sure of Katrine either.

"He is very sexy, my Gaultier!" Katrine said.

I turned away, tired of this conversation.

"Jules! I wanted to make sure that you and I were friends first. If you knew how... charming he could be."

I had to say this ranked right up there as one of the stupidest conversations I'd ever heard, let alone had.

"Does Gaultier know you're giving away the store to me?" I asked.

"We often give away free samples. But that is not the point, Jules. I want you to know that this is not the reason I befriended you."

"I thought you just got through telling me it *was*."

"Yes, well, okay, it *was*. But what I really want is for us to be friends."

"As long as I don't sleep with Gaultier."

"Were...were you considering that?"

"Jeez, Katrine! I just laid eyes on him this morning!"

"He is handsome, *n'est-ce pas*?"

"You're safe," I said firmly as I reached my front door. "Go home. And as much as it pains me to say it, stop giving me cheese. I swear on my life you will never find me and Gaultier together." I turned and pushed open the heavy door and allowed it to close again cutting off Katrine's profuse thanks.

I took a second to gather my thoughts in the stairwell since I hadn't had a chance to do that during the walk to the apartment. I slipped my hand into my pocket to touch both metal discs and felt my resolve hardening.

Now that I knew who had killed Lilou I only needed to know why. And then I needed to make sure that Luc heard the truth. I needed a confession. If the evidence wasn't solid enough to convince Luc then the killer would go free and I would be living under the same roof with a murderer. It would only be a matter of time before that murderer took steps to eliminate me and all that I knew once and for all.

That's what *I'd* do if I were a psycho killer.

That's what any sane psycho killer would do.

I hurried up the stairs, my heart pounding in anticipation and tried to steady my breathing. I hesitated at the Madame Twins' door and set the bag of cheese there. If for whatever reason I got thrown off a balcony in the next hour, at least they'd have some Gouda.

I plucked the grocery list from the bag and turned to Merci's apartment door, took in a long breath, and knocked.

23

Dead to Rights

"Hey, Jules," Merci said when she opened the door. "What's up? Is everything okay?"

I didn't answer right away because I was a little taken aback by her innocent-looking face and wide eyes, still pretending we were great pals and all was right with the world.

A part of me just wanted to punch her.

Even though I didn't say a word there was clearly something on *my* face that made Merci realize I might know more than I should. It was like one of those live action scenes where her face just magically melted from cheerful sweetness to hardened evil in one animated swipe.

I pushed past her and entered the living room. It was tidy and very white. I realized I'd never been in her place before.

"What's up, Jules?" Merci asked again only this time there was an edge to her voice.

I held out the grocery note.

"You wrote this," I said.

Her eyes flickered to the note but she made no move to take it. "Okay," she said.

"I have another note you wrote too," I said. "Only that one was delivered via the crack under my front door."

I pulled the note out of my pocket and dangled it in front of her, mindful in case she tried to snatch it away.

"I'm confused," Merci said as she walked over to stand between the living room and the kitchen. She held a dishcloth in her hand.

"Let me spell it out. You wrote me a threatening note telling me to stop investigating Lilou Basso's death or I'd be the next one killed."

"If you say so, Jules."

"You can stop lying, Merci. I *know* you wrote the threatening note. In fact I've already shown it to the police."

Merci shrugged. "You can't prove I wrote that note. I can't imagine DeBray took prints from it."

"He didn't have to. The handwriting in the note matches this grocery list perfectly."

"Who's to say *I* wrote that grocery list? Did you see me write it?"

"It's signed by you! Plus I saw you write the note to your mother yesterday that you put on your door so I can testify that this is your handwriting."

"Testify?" Merci barked out a laugh. "Do you think we are a television crime show? You can't prove any of this."

"You think you're off the hook because there's no more DNA to confirm evidence but there are other ways to prove you wrote this. Expert handwriting analyst's opinions are considered admissible in a court of law. I barely made it through my undergraduate classes at university but even I can tell these two notes were written in the same handwriting. A jury will see it too."

"What difference does it make? Even if you did somehow get this to court—a big if by the way—and even if everyone agreed I'd written a note saying *you're next* or whatever, that isn't a crime! In an apocalyptic world? You really think anyone gives a crap about poison pen letters when people are looting and killing to survive?"

"First, there's no indication it will get that bad here in France and second, yeah, I think people will always want justice. They'll always want to know that if you kill someone, you'll pay a price for it. And as for you trying to warn me off looking for Lilou's killer? *Any* jury—even one of *your* peers which admittedly would be pretty stupid—will see the handwriting on the wall so to speak."

Merci laughed. "You can't possibly think *I* killed Lilou! You said yourself that the police said she was strangled! Look at me! Lilou outweighed me by fifty pounds!"

"First I'm positive I never told you how Lilou was killed and second, I'm not accusing you of killing her," I said.

"Well, it sure sounded like it."

"I'm accusing you of protecting her killer. Your brother. Guy."

An abrupt sound came from the bedroom which was behind me but I didn't turn to look because all I needed to see was the look of triumph on Merci's face as she looked over my shoulder.

"I am being sorry about this, Jules," Guy said in a low threatening voice.

24

When Push Comes to Shove

Guy moved quickly from the doorway of the bedroom to the front door where he stood and faced me. And blocked my exit route.

"I am so sorry," Guy said again and if I had to swear to it in a court of law I'd have to say he really did look sorry.

Unfortunately that's probably exactly how he looked as he was choking the life out of Lilou Basso.

I know it sounds trite but at the time all I could do was blurt out, "You won't get away with this!"

"Get away with what?" Merci sneered. "You think anybody cares about you? You are just one more obnoxious tourist and worse because it was *your* country that did this to us!"

"You don't know that," I said, hoping to stall for time, although I wasn't at all sure why I thought that would help me.

"The Americans start all the problems. Everybody knows that."

"Did the Americans kill Lilou?"

"It doesn't matter. Nobody will care when your body ends up in the canal."

"Going to vary things this time? Afraid if you bury me in the garden Luc will figure it out?"

"Oh it's *Luc*, is it? I should have known. But it doesn't matter. Just like you said, the police have their hands full with other problems."

"That was *you* at the canal, wasn't it? You pushed me in. How did you know I would be there? You weren't even in the *boulangerie* when Jim told me about it."

I gave a silent apology to Jim for suspecting him. If I survived this day I'd be sure and make it up to him somehow.

Please God let me have the chance to make it up to him.

"This is a village, remember? After you left, my mother went into the *boulangerie* and Madame Fournier gossiped to her about *the American woman* who was just in there heading out to the canal. I met my mother a few minutes later on the street and she told me I needed to take care of you for Guy's sake."

"Your *mother's* in on this too?"

"What did you think? That we wouldn't protect him? Is that how they do things in your country? In your family?"

I looked at Guy. He was a big man but right now he was wringing his hands and looking at Merci for instructions.

"Wow," I said. "You're a lucky man, Guy. Mind you, between you, your mother and your crazy sister, any woman you marry should probably sleep with a knife under her pillow."

"Shut up!" Merci snarled, snatching up a butcher knife from the kitchen counter as if I'd just given her the idea. "You don't know anything about us."

"Thank God for small favors," I muttered but I kept my eyes on the knife.

"Merci, *non*," Guy said. "Too messy!"

I nearly lost my lunch at that, I have to tell you, and I hadn't had lunch yet so you can see how bad things were.

Stall! Stall!

"Why?" I said to Guy, trying not to look at Merci's knife and hoping Guy would prevent her from making a mess. "Why did you do it?"

Guy's shoulders slumped. "It was an accident. I didn't mean to hurt her."

I nodded as if I knew how traumatizing it must have been for him, but strangling was a slow death. It may or may not have been premeditated, but it was *no* accident.

❈❈❈❈❈

Luc knew he smelled to high heaven. But he also knew he couldn't dismiss the necessary attentions of the rescued boy's mother. What was it the mayor had said to Luc just this morning?

Half of this EMP problem is really a PR problem.

So when he'd returned little Gaston to his *maman*—who had smacked the child around the ears for the trouble he'd caused—and she insisted that Luc stay for a cup of coffee and hear the thanks of both parents, he knew he had no alternative.

The bath would wait. Reassuring the good people of Chabanel that life would go on in spite of the EMP and that it could still be good—*that* was a message that needed delivering, one family at time perhaps or even one person at a time.

As Gaston's mother poured Luc's coffee and chattered on about how Monsieur would be home any minute or perhaps at the top of the hour at the latest, Luc allowed himself to rest and mentally turn off for a few minutes.

The problems of Chabanel would always be there waiting for him—and they would be never ceasing. But for now, for this afternoon, Luc didn't have to solve them all.

He closed his eyes and felt the day's weariness pour over him as the aroma of the freshly brewed coffee and the satisfaction of a job well-done cascaded over him.

Je suis désolé, Lilou, he thought resignedly.

I can't do it all.

And for one perfect moment, he really believed that.

※※※※※

I stood there, sweat forming on my top lip, my heart pounding trying to gauge the distance between the front door and where Guy stood. I wasn't too worried about Mercy. I was pretty sure I could knock her out of my way if I got enough momentum going but I would have to outmaneuver Guy.

Because once he got a hand on me, I was done.

"Don't bother telling her anything, Guy," Merci said to him. "What's the point?"

"I want her to know," Guy said. "I want her to understand that it wasn't my fault." He turned to me. "I knew Lilou. I've known her since she was in grade school."

I was working very hard to think, to keep an eye on Merci—clearly the bat-shit crazy wild card in the equation—and to look like I was listening sympathetically. Very tricky since I was not only scared to death of Guy but intensely repulsed by him too.

"We were together and I knew she wanted to...you know, be together in the sex way, yes?"

I nodded encouragingly as if I was not just about to vomit all down the front of my Saint Laurent silk blouse.

"But then she was saying *non!* and getting loud, you see? We did not have the sex but I had done some things—"

"Oh, for heaven's sakes, Guy!" Merci said in frustration. "It doesn't matter! And telling *her* means nothing! *She* won't forgive you! *She* can't forgive you."

I looked at Merci and I know the fear was etched across my face. Merci may be classic straight-jacket material but she had a clearer view of the situation than Guy did.

"Lilous's father is crazy," Merci said to me in a bored voice. "If she'd told him what she and Guy had gotten up to, he'd have come after Guy. Guy would have to watch his back every minute of every day right up until the moment the old bastard finally drove a knife between his ribs."

"You killed Lilou so she wouldn't tell her father?" I said to Guy.

He nodded, his eyes wide and hopeful that I would see the pragmatic logic of it all.

"It was a moment of weakness," he said beseechingly.

Yeah, followed by at least ten minutes of determined, murderous effort. Strangling isn't a crime of passion. It takes too long. Your victim's face is between your hands the whole time. Guy had plenty of time to stop and come to his senses.

Something he had not done.

"Feel better now?" Merci said sarcastically to Guy.

"I just wanted someone to know," he said sadly.

"So now she knows," Merci said pointing her knife at me. "But if I were in her shoes I wouldn't be thanking you."

"Merci, *non!*" Guy said, waving the knife away.

My heart rose at the thought that Guy would not let this happen. He would not allow his crazy-ass sister to chase me around the living room with a butcher knife.

I was just about to thank him when he turned to Merci and said sadly, "Let me take her to the bedroom and do it quietly."

Oh hell no. Cue the *not doing it quietly* part of the program.

I started screaming.

25

Free Falling

I saw the sun glinting off the wrought iron railing on the balcony but I couldn't take eyes off the two people slowly edging toward me from both sides.

The time for conversation was over. I don't know what I expected when I came here to confront Merci but ending up fighting for my life was definitely not one of them.

Why didn't I realize how desperate she'd be? What made me think she'd just crumble and confess? Because she'd been so friendly to me up to now?

Even Ted Bundy was charming in social situations.

With two against one I knew that unless flinging myself off the balcony was an option it was only a matter of time before they grabbed me.

I vowed I wouldn't go easy.

I saw Guy's move before he made it and instead of ducking him when he lunged at me, I jumped on the couch and slammed my elbow into his face. A spurt of blood jettisoned out of his nose and Merci screamed, "My couch!"

Bitch.

As I tried to jump away, still screaming my head off, Guy wrapped both arms around my hips and pulled me into his chest.

"For God's sakes, shut her up, Guy!" Merci yelled.

He grabbed my arms and pinned them to my side and I felt the desperation build up inside me as I struggled uselessly in his grasp.

I took in a huge intake of breath to let out another ear-piercing scream—which I never got to do—but that long inhalation probably saved my life.

Just before I was about to let loose a monster scream, Guy slapped a meaty hand firmly across my nose and mouth.

And then the door erupted in loud pounding.

I held my breath behind Guy's hand and renewed my efforts to squirm free but he picked me up as if he were collecting the trash and ran into the kitchen.

"Hurry!" Merci hissed at him as she went to the door.

Guy moved into the part of the kitchen not visible by the front door. With his giant hand completely covering my nose and mouth I began to see sparks and dots as I fought for air.

"Answer the door!" Guy said hoarsely to Merci. I began to twitch and struggle violently as I fought for breath, but a part of me needed to hear what was happening at the door.

My heart sank and a heaviness infused my body as I heard the tremulous tone of one of the old ladies from next door. Only in my wildest, most desperate dreams did I think it might be Luc.

And now all was truly lost.

Just as I willed myself to stop struggling and let the worst happen, I felt Guy loosen his grip on my mouth and I took in a loud and wracking suck of air into my lungs.

He dropped me completely then and while I was trying to gasp in bigger and bigger gulps of air, I groped on the floor for anything I could use to fight back with—a knife, a heavy pan, a dish of cat kibble—when I heard one of the old ladies speaking.

I looked up and saw two things I'm sure I will never see again in this lifetime.

I saw Guy looking at his feet in the picture of contrition and shame.

And I saw Madame Becque, a frail ninety-two year old woman, holding a German Luger aimed at Guy's chest. Behind her Merci was sitting on the floor in the living room with a stunned look on her face.

The other twin stood over Merci and held a very old rifle to her head. Madame Cazaly peered into the kitchen at me. When we got eye contact, Madame C gave me the first smile I'd ever received from her.

And as I would learn later, it was the first smile she'd given anyone in nearly fifty years.

26

When You Least Expect It

There's nothing like catching the killer of an innocent girl to make the locals decide to treat you to free coffee and croissants.

I was sitting in my usual spot at Café Sucre where I'd been hanging out for the last two weeks since uncovering Lilou Basso's killer, just sitting and drinking my free coffee and trying to imagine how my life had changed drastically in such a short time.

First, I'd heard from Thibault who, let me just say right now, is actually a very sweet man and someone I actually look forward to seeing now. Thibault reported that things looked to be settling down in the States and for that I was immensely grateful.

While for me the idea of *settling down* suggested that I might soon be able to use my airline points to get back home, Luc assured me it merely meant fewer people were being shot and eaten back home.

That Luc. What a card.

Solving Lilou Basso's murder could have caused a rift between me and Luc for a lot of different reasons, not just because it was me, a foreigner who solved it or because he'd specifically told me to butt out and I hadn't.

But also because if not for the Madame Twins and their illegal arsenal of World War II guns and ammo I'd come really close to being Murder Victim Number Two.

Fortunately, none of that mattered now. Apart from the initial shock at finding two old ladies armed to the teeth and me on the verge of hysteria—it had been a very trying afternoon—Luc had taken it all in stride.

He got everyone's statement, locked up the appropriate people, scolded the old ladies for their gun hoarding while he praised them for saving the day, and spent a chaste night on my couch to ensure that I felt safe and secure from the stressful day's events.

All in all, very nice.

It wasn't just the matching handwriting that put it all together for me. In fact, if Thibault hadn't tossed down a washer that looked just like the one I'd discovered in the garden where Lilou was killed, I might not have made the connection.

But when I saw that little metal disc I suddenly remembered all the junk on the counter in Thibault's apartment. I remembered Guy idly looking through it—as he would since he and Thibault were both mechanical fix-it kind of guys.

Then when I realized the handwriting matched up and knew that Merci was somehow involved I also knew the killer who'd left behind part of the contents of his pocket had to be connected to her.

Voila, as they say around here.

Guy accommodated everyone by confessing to killing Lilou and while Luc was playing it cagey vis-à-vis what would happen to him, it seemed sure that Guy would be punished. I didn't know whether France had the death penalty but the way Guy had brutally killed poor Lilou I figured he was a slam dunk for the guillotine.

But hey. That's probably just me.

Honestly, the biggest shock of all was the Madame Twins riding to my rescue, bugles blaring. It seemed they'd heard my screams and began to flashback to a time when *le bosch* could make anyone in the village scream like that.

When they came to Merci's door, their guns out and both of them ready to rumble, they were astonished to see that Merci was not only *not* in any kind of trouble as they'd assumed, but was in fact covering for the monster they could see reflected in the dull but still mirror-like refrigerator surface who was holding a struggling and quickly expiring American in his grip.

"You have not left from that spot since yesterday!"

I looked up to see Luc DeBray striding toward me, a grin on his face that did weird but pleasurable things to my insides. He kissed me on both cheeks and signaled to the waiter before pulling up a chair to join me.

"That's right," I said. "This is my new home." I waved a hand to encompass the café tables and chairs, some with umbrellas to protect against the growing harshness of the afternoon sun.

"I see. Have you decided how you are going to make a living?" he asked.

"Wow. You get right to it, don't you? Isn't there any reward money or something for finding Lilou's killer?"

"*Non*. You did that as a concerned citizen, of course. The village of Chabanel thanks you."

"Okay, well. You're welcome."

"Besides, do I not take care of you?" he smiled slyly at me and I honestly did not know how to react. It was true Luc came over to my apartment most evenings and he never came empty-handed. More than half the time the Madame Twins were there too. As lovely as those nights were, surely he didn't think I could live on the grace of his handouts forever?

"I thought about it and I'm going to try to be a private eye," I said.

"I am not knowing this phrase."

"I'm going to be a private detective. You know, because you're so slammed."

"*Slammed*?"

"Because you're so busy. I would be helping you solve crimes in Chabanel."

"*Non*. This I do not want. Besides, you don't speak French."

"I'll get an interpreter until I can figure it out myself."

"This is *un désastre*."

"I honestly think it makes a lot of sense," I said cheerfully as the waiter put Luc's coffee in front of him.

I have to say I'd been thinking about this a lot in the two weeks since my confrontation with Mercy and Guy.

The fact was while I hated the *reason* for doing it, I'd quite enjoyed the work itself of talking to people in order to find out the truth. It seemed to me that with all the Americans trapped in Aix and probably other little French villages in Provence too—not to mention the fact that Luc had his hands full with the apocalypse—sleuthing as a profession might be just the thing for me.

"I was a reporter back in the States," I said. "So I know all about questioning people and following leads."

"I thought you said you wrote about movies for your paper."

"I was in line for a promotion," I said defensively. "But the point is, I was *trained* to be an investigative reporter. I have the skills to question people and then follow a line of inquiry. And I think I've demonstrated that I can follow an investigation to its conclusion."

"No one will pay you for this."

"I disagree. Someone who's being railroaded would. Someone who wants to prove their innocence would. Someone who wants justice when the cops are too busy to do the legwork would."

"I see. And what will you do when one of your clients pays you with a live lamb? Or a bushel of lavender? Or perhaps the offer to paint your living room instead of something you can actually use?"

"I don't know, Luc. I guess I'll figure it out as I go."

Luc snorted and shook his head. I think he probably knew he couldn't forbid me from doing it and he probably thought there was every reason to believe I'd lose interest after the first squawking chicken I got handed by a grateful client.

But whatever the reason, I had the irresistible feeling that I'd just mentally put up a shingle.

I'm in the private eye business.
In France.
During the apocalypse.

Boy, my sales brochures were going to be killer.

Over Luc's shoulder I spotted Katrine and her husband loading up a single horse drawn wagon with what was left of their cheese from the morning's market.

After things had calmed down a little, I'd made a point to pull Katrine aside and apologize for what had to seem like a very harsh dismissal of her confession to me two weeks earlier.

She was cool with it and I have to chalk that up to the fact that, in spite of her fears, she needed a friend. And while I wasn't going to be turning down any offers of free cheese—*hey, the old ladies like cheese too you know and it wouldn't be fair to them*—I couldn't help but feel there was a connection between me and Katrine that would serve us both well in the years to come.

God. Was I really going to be stuck over here for years?

Luc's girl sergeant hurried to the table and spoke quickly to him in French. She glanced at me from time to time as she spoke and I was reminded that she and Merci had been sort of friends. I'm not sure what she thought of me—it was so hard to tell with the French—but she didn't look like she wanted to give me any free cheese.

"I must go," Luc said, standing and swallowing the last of his coffee. "Movies tonight?"

"Ha, ha," I said. "Funny guy. But yeah, come by if you're free. The Madame Twins are telling stories of the war tonight."

"I wouldn't miss it." He leaned over and kissed me again and was gone.

I watched him disappear and tried to assimilate how I felt about him. I was determined to do everything I could not to fall in love with him. If I had any control over these things. In the meantime, I would enjoy his friendship and his company.

I glanced at my watch and saw that I'd be late for my engagement if I didn't hurry. I'd promised Jim that I'd go over an article he'd written for the Chabanel paper this afternoon.

Some time after the whole Lilou mess got sorted out with Guy and Merci, Jim came to me and told me exactly why he'd lied about Lilou. The fact that he hadn't made me track him down to hear the truth was in his favor.

Still. Lying. Not good for any relationship. At any stage.

It turned out that Jim had a sister back in the States who was mentally challenged and he said he somehow felt less guilty about her when he spent time with Lilou. He only ever bought Lilou ice cream or occasionally walked her home but after she was killed, he knew how it would look.

Again, a perfectly good excuse but I still didn't love the whole lying-to-my-face thing. On the other hand I recognized that this new world of ours was also a new world of second chances. I figured if I was going to get mine I shouldn't have a problem with letting Jim have his too.

Beyond that, well, we would just have to see.

<<<◇>>>

To see what happens next to Jules and life in post-apocalyptic France, be sure and check out Book 2 in the *Stranded in Provence* Mystery series, *Crimes and Croissants*, available wherever e-books are sold.

ABOUT THE AUTHOR

Susan Kiernan-Lewis lives in Ponte Vedra, Florida and writes mysteries and romantic suspense. Like many authors, Susan depends on the reviews and word of mouth referrals of her readers. If you enjoyed *Parlez-Vous Murder?* please consider leaving a review saying so on Amazon.com, Barnesandnoble.com or Goodreads.com. Check out Susan's website at susankiernanlewis.com and feel free to contact her at sanmarcopress@me.com.

Printed in Great Britain
by Amazon